NICK CARTER
IS IT!

"Nick Carter out-Bonds James Bond."
—*Buffalo Evening News*

"Nick Carter is America's #1 espionage agent."
—*Variety*

"Nick Carter is razor-sharp suspense."
—*King Features*

"Nick Carter is extraordinarily big."
Bestsellers

"Nick Carter has attracted an army of addicted readers . . . the books are fast, have plenty of action and just the right degree of sex . . . Nick Carter is the American James Bond, suave, sophisticated, a killer with both the ladies and the enemy."
—*The New York Times*

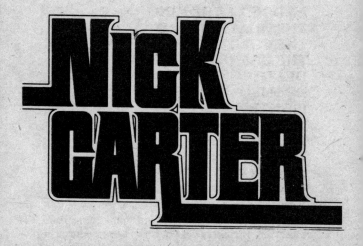

NICK CARTER

THE DUBROVNIK MASSACRE

CHARTER
NEW YORK

A Division of Charter Communications Inc.
A GROSSET & DUNLAP COMPANY
51 Madison Avenue
New York, New York 10010

First Ace Charter Printing July 1981
Published simultaneously in Canada
Manufactured in the United States of America

2 4 6 8 0 9 7 5 3 1

Dedicated to the Men of the Secret
Services of the United States of America

PROLOGUE

"Dusan, you have not let me down. They told me you would refuse to come."

"It's our country I intend not to let down, Josip. Your bureaucrats and lackeys tell me it is urgent."

"You are bitter, Dusan. I put you into prison. You were always loyal, but you strutted around like a little tin god rubbing our noses in our failings. If the Stalinists had won, they would have destroyed both you and our freedom."

"They won when you won, my marshal."

"For fifty years I have kept our nation strong, independent—"

"And what have you achieved? You are as bad as they are. Only the face is different . . . What do you want?"

"I ask that you bury your bitterness and act to save our country. I don't ask your forgiveness."

"Save *our* country? It's always been *your* country. I thought my marshal had already saved *his* country."

"Dusan, listen to me. A conspiracy has reached into the highest circles. They will seize power when I die. There is a timetable—sabotage, civil unrest, bloody riots between our many nationalities.

Chaos. The Red Army will roll over our borders and—"

"That is fantasy. Your mind is going, Josip. They would love an excuse to invade us. They have never forgiven you for taking Yugoslavia out of the Eastern bloc. But for the moment they have no excuse."

"They will be invited."

"By whom? No one wants them."

"Do you know Deijer?"

"One of your hand-picked successors?"

"He is one."

"Impossible! Even we dissidents would have a hard time believing him a traitor."

"Let me explain. He is not KGB, he is a 'controlled one.' There are others at the highest levels. KGB has used them to place agents everywhere, in OZNA, the army, the Party . . . They will assassinate the honest patriots and call in the Red Army to restore order."

"Josip, if you had fought the Stalinists openly, fairly, this would not have happened. They had no mass support. You drove them underground with your phony trials and purges. But I can't believe Deijer—"

"Blackmail."

"But how?"

"Proof, Dusan, proof they collaborated with the Nazis. The Stalinist group CRML found out a few years after I threw out the Russians. They've been working with the KGB to blackmail them for years."

"Josip, are you sure? How do you know?"

"Eduard."

"Surely not!"

"He was one, too, I'm afraid. But he confessed

to me. Copies of the documents are still buried in the mountains. The Nazis had a secret intelligence post there. Eduard gave me a map. You must get these papers and publish them. You are the only one who I can be sure is not one of them. It is up to you. Gather your friends and fight. I will not live to see the week begin again."

"I am old, too, Josip. I walk strangely. Your guards laughed when the legs they broke were set wrong. They also broke my hands. . . . And my wife? What about Maria?"

"That wasn't my doing."

"You had her murdered as a warning."

"They exceeded their orders. They were punished very severely."

"Did it bring her back! You only made more widows. Josip, I know you. You do not love our country as much as your reputation. You will appear a fool if the Red Army crushes us after you die."

"They will kill you and your friends, Dusan."

"I can always flee to the West."

"You won't do that. I know you, Dusan. Here is a complete pardon. Here is the map. If you do this I will issue a statement endorsing you and your friends and commending our country into your hands."

"Josip, I love our country, but spare me your phony promises."

"Dusan, for once be practical! Alone, you and your intellectual friends have little chance."

"Practical?"

"You have Western contacts. Use them. When the time comes, eliminate them or throw them out."

"I have no such contacts."

"You will have to bring them in. Just ask for 'Western technicians.' They'll know what you mean."

"But I don't know anyone!"

"Go see Andrej. He works for them."

"One standard for your son-in-law, but all others are shot."

"Bah! You will never understand, Dusan. You are a worthless, useless, stiff-backed idealist. You have no practicality."

"It's this useless, worthless idealist you are asking to save your country."

"Dusan, the Red Army will destroy everything. The Americans will do anything to keep them from having Mediterranean ports. Don't try and prove how hardheaded you are.

"Remember in the mountains when we fought side by side? You were the one I always had in mind as my successor. But you are stubborn. If we don't get help . . . Promise me, Dusan, promise me. I will make my statement."

"We are both old, my marshal. Maybe . . . I am tired. My idealism runs cooler. It has faded with time just as . . . I fear I shall be joining you before the year—"

"Your answer, Dusan, your answer!"

"You are answered, Josip."

CHAPTER I

It was one of those spring days when Washington looks like the most beautiful city on earth. There aren't many. It takes a lot of beauty to overwhelm the odor of power and money that pervades the city like an unfragrant fog. It would be my luck to spend this particular day indoors at AXE headquarters on Dupont Circle.

It was a day of being poked and prodded, a day of medical tests to see if the body still functioned, psychological tests to see if the brain still had its gearing. It was a day of forms and questionnaires, arguments about expenses with accountants who had never even seen the wrong end of a .22, a day of requisitions and vouchers. They checked everything thoroughly, but what worried them most was the shoulder and the brain.

I've seen a lot of men take a bullet, and that day it had been my turn—a .38 slug at point-blank range in the right shoulder. Nick Carter, AXE Killmaster, had taken a slug in Nairobi. My life was never in danger, but my work was. It took four operations to get that shoulder up to Killmaster specifications.

They sent me to the doctor in Houston, the one

who patches up potentates and dictators. He told me AXE's finest doctors were butchers, but the guy truly had magic fingers. I watched the operation from a mirror he had rigged up. The Houston doctor had greasy glasses, and even through his hospital gown he reeked of expensive Havana cigars. His idea of operating-room chatter was tales of his sexual conquests. He liked butterball blondes with big breasts. It didn't take away from his work one bit. When he got through, the shoulder worked.

They were also worried about the brain. At AXE they don't call it going nuts, they call it crossing the line. They are always afraid that one of us might begin to enjoy the work too much and go into private practice. Going into private practice happened in Nairobi, but it wasn't me. I took a bullet from a "friend." The shrinks thought I'd go nuts over that. They've never been in the field. If I go nuts it will be because I have had to put up with one shrink too many.

I was happier than hell when they finally ushered me into Hawk's office late in the afternoon. Theoretically, it's the managing editor's office of the Amalgamated Press and Wire Service. But what my boss, David Hawk, actually does is manage AXE. There's only one man in the country he reports to.

I wondered what was up. I had "accidentally" run into one of my language instructors in the hallway. We just "happened" to strike up a conversation in Serbo-Croatian. I figured I was headed for Yugoslavia, and that didn't seem so bad. Yugoslavia has a secret police, OZNA, but compared to KGB they are almost sweethearts. Besides, I liked

Yugoslavia. I even liked the marshal, who was not a bad tyrant as tyrants went. Also, if there is any language I speak absolutely like a native in four or five dialects, it is Serbo-Croatian.

Hawk wasn't home. They told me he would be with me in a minute. That wasn't like him, but the office was the same. Everything was exactly where I remembered it. Even the chair I sat in felt the same. The office smelled, not faintly, of Hawk's cheap cigars. I took out one of my gold monogrammed cigarettes and lit up. I hadn't been smoking much lately. Slows the recovery.

When Hawk came in, he looked as wiry and tough as ever. And I thought then, as I have often thought: I have never seen a man his age keep himself in better shape. But if he looked the same, his manner was different. Hawk was definitely upset. He paced back and forth behind his desk like a father expecting quintuplets. I had seen him worried during an operation when everything was going wrong, but I had never seen him this way before an operation had even begun. He said nothing for a couple of minutes. Then he stopped behind his desk and looked at me coldly.

"Okay, N3, stand up." I got up but I was uneasy.

"Let's see Hugo." There was some embarrassment in his voice.

Hugo is my stiletto. With a flick of my wrist Hugo slid out of his sheath on my left arm and into my hand. As a bonus I pulled back my coat and showed him Wilhelmina, my 9mm luger, tucked under my left armpit. I didn't show him Pierre, the small gas bomb taped to my thigh. But not because I was shy. I knew why he had asked about Hugo.

Hawk figured I could fool the doctors but knew I would never carry Hugo where I couldn't reach him quickly, even in AXE's office.

"Okay, N3, sit down." Hawk sat down, too, but on the edge of his chair, like a kid watching an adventure movie. "You're too damn patriotic for your own good, N3. I can't send you on this one with a clipped wing." He paused a minute. "Have you heard of Dusan Ankevic?"

Ankevic was the Yugoslav dissident who had once been the marshal's right-hand man. He had broken with the old man in 1950 over the lack of human rights, and had been in and out of the marshal's prisons ever since.

"Yes, sir," I said. "Even read one of his books once."

"I suppose you're as impressed with this guy as everyone else. Don't see it myself. Damn plaster saint, although . . ." Hawk gestured to a cable, which he placed on his desk.

"Well, he is tough," I said. "They broke his hands so he couldn't write. He kept writing. Broke his legs, killed his wife. But I don't think—"

"You're going to say they never broke Ankevic. Am I right?" Hawk interrupted.

I started to reply, but Hawk began again. "He is a pacifist, right? You seem to know a lot about him, N3."

"Well, not absolutely nonviolent, but he certainly wouldn't have anything to do with the likes of us."

Hawk permitted himself a grin, but only for a moment.

"He just has. He approached a CIA contact in Belgrade a few days ago and said he needs the help of a Western 'technician' right away."

"That surprises me, sir. He is as rigid about keeping Yugoslavia out of the hands of the East or West as the marshal. Are they sure it was actually Ankevic?"

"The Company's contact has known him personally for years. Ankevic went to the CIA."

"It still surprises me, sir."

"It surprises everyone, N3. It surprises the Man." My ears pricked up at the mention of the Man; they're supposed to. It tells me how high up the matter has gone.

Hawk went on. "Ankevic couldn't just want out, since he could easily leave. They would be glad to be rid of him. The answer is obvious, or so they tell me. The old boy wants to settle a few scores. He wants somebody killed. What else could 'Western technician' mean? He doesn't want a computer programmer, for Christ's sake!"

"That doesn't sound like him, sir."

"Actually, I agree with you, N3. But the bright boys can't think of anything else. But there is something else. About a week ago he had a secret meeting with the Fox."

"The marshal, sir?"

"Yes."

"As stubborn as both men are, it's hard to believe they got together just to talk about old times. That meeting cost them both a lot of pride."

"I think you're right." He paused for several seconds and looked at his cable again. "I am convinced something ominous has happened. You see, I have been watching the Fox closely. As long as the Fox wasn't worried about what happened when he kicked off, neither was I. Nick, about ten days ago, very suddenly, the Fox got worried. I won't go into the details, but it looked for a while like he had another purge up his sleeve. Then suddenly he stopped dead in his tracks, like he knew his plans wouldn't work. For two long days he did nothing. Then he called Ankevic and set up the meeting. He must have learned something so dangerous to Yugoslavia that he was forced to call his oldest and most bitter enemy for help. That's my analysis. The damn thing is I'm also convinced the Company had the meeting bugged and is holding out on us."

"Why would they do that, sir?"

"I'll explain in a minute, N3. But maybe some background on the conflict would help.

"I have followed the Fox's career for years. He is the last of the great ones from World War II. Churchill, Roosevelt, De Gaulle, Stalin—they're all dead. Only the Fox remains. Now he's on his death bed. There is a lot of talk about resistance movements, but the Fox's partisans were the best. They killed more Nazis than the rest of the resistance groups put together. Why, the Fox tied down twelve crack German divisions in Yugoslavia. But, hell, you know most of this."

He started pacing back and forth, his hands clasped behind his back.

I did, but I listened respectfully as Hawk warmed to his subject. I knew what the Fox meant to him. He had stood up for the Fox years ago when it wasn't popular. The Company had even tried to label him a Commie sympathizer and it had almost cost him his career. But Hawk didn't know I knew the story. Besides, I respect the fact that Hawk explains things to his men. Some of the bright boys treat us like dogs; we're supposed to chomp whoever they point at and not ask questions.

Hawk lit up a new cigar and began puffing away with obvious satisfaction. "The Fox is a Commie, of course, but he's a patriotic Commie. By 1948 he was fed up with Stalin and the Red Army, so he kicked them out. They have never, never forgiven him. Now that he's about to kick off, it's the Soviets' big chance to undo everything the Fox did to them and also gain ports in the Mediterranean. The whole balance of power in Europe would shift in their favor.

"There has been a battle in government for years about how we should deal with the Fox. I took one side, the Company the other. I have always respected the Fox, even though he's a Commie. I have always argued that we should leave him alone. How these fools in the Company think they can teach the Fox any tricks, I don't know. It's like a bunch of damn grasshoppers deciding they can teach a lion to roar. Why, the Fox has kicked more KGB personnel in the ass than all the Western intelligence agencies put together. The idiots never understood the Fox. Everyone admires Ankevic; it would be hypocritical for the head of the AXE to admire him too. Hell, the Fox is the one I admire.

"Anyway, I argued that we should leave the Fox's succession to the Fox. Keep our paws off. And, N3, the Man sided with me."

"Sounds like a fairy-tale ending," I said.

"That's just it. It didn't end there. The Company wanted this one bad, but he gave it to us. Bad blood. The Company says we're an anachronism. They want us either cut back or brought under their wing. They implied we were a bunch of thugs.

Hell, at least when we kill somebody we get the right person. You know they tried to kill Ankevic themselves years ago and blamed it on the Fox. Claimed the Fox was going to have him murdered anyway. Killed some poor slob in the Yugoslav foreign office by mistake. Damn it, Nick, they get more people killed in one of their stupid coups than we've murdered in thirty years.

"I'm way out on a limb on this one, N3. The Man is generous but unforgiving. If the Red Army comes rolling into Yugoslavia after I convinced him to leave well enough alone, it will be the end of AXE. The Company is just waiting for our number to be up. One thing is certain. You're not going to get any help on this one. The Company is going to play hardball. Stay away from Company personnel. In fact, stay away from AXE personnel. You're going in there solo and you're going in there blind. I'll give you a couple of names and numbers, but that's it."

"I understand," I said.

"I thought you would, N3, which is why I've chosen you. It looks like a tough one."

The feud with the Company didn't surprise me all that much. There is no man in the world I admire more than David Hawk. He is a great leader. But put him in a committee meeting and he turns into an animal. It's kill or be killed. He has no more mercy for the CIA than for the KGB. If they make a mistake he rubs their noses in it. Hawk has made enemies.

"Why not send in a dozen agents?" I asked.

"That's just it. The Man himself has spoken. A direct order. Ankevic asked for only one man. We send only one man. We must show respect. The

Man thinks that plaster puffball is the next best thing to cream cheese. You know how he gets about this human rights stuff. It's a damn obsession with him. No, Nick, you're it."

"I can handle it."

"You're walking into a killing ground. It's not just OZNA and KGB. There is a secret Stalinist group, CRML. And there's a bunch of neo-Nazis who call themselves the Blood of Croatia. We have unconfirmed reports they are planning to assassinate dissidents and liberals. Oh, one last thing. The Fox wouldn't have gone to Ankevic unless he had just one shot. That's all you'll have, N3, one shot. Fail, and Yugoslavia goes."

"I have a friend in the Company, sir. Perhaps I could get a copy—"

"I don't want to know about it, N3. That's up to you."

Hawk got up and went to his safe. In a minute he was back, file in hand. He handed me the file and an airline ticket. The file didn't have much in it, background and details of the meeting. There were photos of Ankevic. He looked as impressive as the biography made him sound: lean, ascetic face; high, broad forehead; chiseled mouth. The later photos showed the pain. He had been hurt in the Fox's prisons, hurt badly. The details of the meeting were very bad; obviously they were amateurs. I didn't complain. I leave complaining to accountants.

I gave Hawk back the file and kept the ticket. I was leaving for Belgrade that evening. Hawk walked around in front of his desk. He stood less than a foot from me.

"You know not to get taken alive, N3; you have

your capsule for that. On this mission, though, you can't afford to be taken dead either. The Man doesn't want these dissidents discredited. I promised him it wouldn't happen." He took a small object in his hand, a bomb only slightly larger than Pierre. "If it looks like the end of the line, take this in both hands and hold it up to your face." He showed me how to use it.

"Anti-identification grenade?"

"Yeah," he said grimly. No fingerprints, no dental work. It's powerful. Probably won't be anything left of you bigger than an eyeball. But it's best to use it the right way."

"I won't hesitate."

"Good. I want you to use this thing even if you're in a room filled with schoolchildren." Hawk then casually dropped the bomb into my lap and walked back behind his desk.

"What will you call this one?" he said.

"Waldo, I think, sir. I use him to shoot the whole wad."

"Sounds good. One more thing. Apparently Ankevic has this thing against smoking. Brother died of lung cancer. Took a long time going. Can you give it up for the duration?"

"I did it when I took a bullet in the lung."

"Good. Many men would die for their country but wouldn't give up their smoking habit for it." He reached out his hand. "Good luck, N3."

"I'll keep the Fox's handiwork together," I said as I left. But he was already lost in thought and didn't appear to hear me.

CHAPTER II

I made my way out of AXE offices as quickly as I could. To the staff these offices are a kind of home—familiar, reassuring, secure. To me they are just rooms. I have never been behind most of the closed doors. Most of the faces are new, sleek, self-satisfied. Only the security checks are exactly as they have always been.

The world outside looked great, green and new, yet mellow in the late-afternoon light. But right then I had a phone call to make, quickly. That I walked three blocks to a drugstore pay phone before doing so is a tribute to those new faces at AXE headquarters. I called Jerry Goldstein, a friend who worked for the Company. Jerry worked just four blocks from AXE. I had never met him there. Jerry and I traded information. It's not strictly Kosher, but then both Jerry and I preferred staying alive to playing by the rules.

Luckily, Jerry was in. I told him what I needed. He wasn't sure he could get it, but wanted me to meet him right away anyway. He was worried. He wouldn't say why, even though his phone had a scrambler on it. He said something about my not getting mad about the money they said I owed on the car. I didn't owe any money. I said thanks and hung up. In the movies everything is always clear; for a Killmaster it seldom is. I didn't know how far the Company would go.

Most people have no idea how sleazy it gets a few blocks from the White House. We were to meet a dozen blocks east and north at a porno theater. The neighborhood is bad. But there are a lot of middle-class guys on the street because of all the action that goes on. It was a nice day. I decided to walk over. Besides, I couldn't take my car, not with the Company being involved. AXE would take care of the car after I was out of town. I cut across town feeling pretty good.

When I arrived at the theater Jerry wasn't there. I took my usual seat and waited. There was much huffing and puffing up on the screen, and the actors looked like they might be enjoying it. As far as I could see, they might as well have been sawing wood. I waited. The next film was no better. And the color quality was worse. Jerry had still not shown. That wasn't like him. I slipped out the side exit to the vacant lot in back of the theater that we use as a back-up spot. I had a bad feeling. Friend Jerry was there, all right, lying face down. His whole back was becoming one red stain. I reached down and touched him. He was still warm, but there was no pulse. His pistol was gone and so was his wallet. I checked his suit pockets; there were no papers. Things don't work out like in the movies.

I walked down the block and phoned the cops.

It was safest now to stay on foot. I walked over to the Capitol building, then turned and walked down the mall toward the Washington Monument. The trees were just as green and pretty as before

Jerry got blown away. I had about half an hour until AXE agents dropped me a "secure" car around the block from the State Department, the area they call foggy bottom.

I stopped on the grassy knoll at the base of the Washington Monument. I thought of the kind of patriotism Jerry represented. I paused a moment, then walked down the hill to Constitution Avenue. Patriotism leads you to strange places. I waited for the stop light. It's always hard to get across Constitution Avenue at rush hour, even for a Killmaster.

A few minutes later, I reached the car, parked just where it was supposed to be, across Twenty-first Street and Virginia Avenue. There are many degrees of secure cars and this was the most secure AXE had. It was an old 1969 Chevy Malibu, picked to be inconspicuous. I started to walk around to the driver's side. On the way I glanced at the hood. I didn't bother getting in. Every once in a while the Company surprises you. I still don't know if they killed Jerry, but this was a message to AXE, loud and clear. The car was shot up and useless.

I looked around. There was nothing to see. I started walking. A couple of blocks away I tossed the useless key into a street drain. I headed for the subway, hoping this was the last surprise of my Washington stay. I don't like subways, but they're easier for losing people than a taxi. As subways go, Washington's is not bad, more like San Francisco's BART than like New York's ugly system.

I walked out of the station and into a brief thunderstorm. By the time I had walked two blocks my jacket and shoes had been washed clean and the rain had stopped.

* * *

Her name was Roberta Ann Fixx. The name
doesn't fit, which is why everybody calls her Strawberry. She is sweet, succulent like her name, but
there is another reason for it—her long,
strawberry-blond hair. Her skin is as white and
translucent as a painted Madonna's, but freckled
lightly like some delicate bird's egg. She is what the
French call une femme honnête—an honest woman—and I respect her for it. She works as a secretary during the day for some do-gooder outfit that
pays worse than the Feds. With her beautiful ass
and her long, strawberry-blond hair she could earn
a thousand dollars a night on the diplomatic party
circuit; but that's not her style. Truckers are her
style, truckers and, although she doesn't know it,
Killmasters.

She lives only a few blocks from where I got off
the subway, across from Rock Creek Park. You
can believe how I hurried. My hands were shaking
by the time I reached the door. Strawberry is so
beautiful that men have died before she got around
to slipping off her panties. I had a problem though:
I was running late. We had time for dinner but not
for loving.

We had a long-standing reservation to Washington's fine French restaurant San Souci, only a
block from the White House. Strawberry had been
looking forward to eating there "forever." We had
to hurry.

I was an hour late, and she was not ready. Wom-
en are never ready. She looked gorgeous. All she
had on was a short slip with matching pale-blue
panties, like you see in those expensive lingerie ads.
I explained we had to hurry, I had a plane to catch.

No time for loving, only for Sans Souci. She had wanted to go there a long time. "Forget it," she said. She smiled. Sometimes when she smiles I think she has ten thousand teeth, all beautiful. She plopped down on the end of her pale-blue silk quilt on her bed and crossed her legs underneath her. She motioned me over. I said we would have to hurry. She said, "Don't worry." That was all she said in the next two hours that bears repeating.

She undid my belt and gently brushed her long, tapered fingers across the fly of my pants. She tossed back her long, strawberry-blond hair and looked up at me. Her eyes were ten shades bluer than her panties. She unzipped my pants and ran two fingers along the bulge in my briefs. I could see the window, reflected in the mirror above her head. I saw a double reflection; the stars were rising high in the east and so was Nick Carter. I saw her lovely pink tongue between her beautiful teeth. Like Sans Souci her appetizers were as delicious as the main courses.

Strawberry likes her loving the way she likes her work: hard, fast, and efficient. She likes to turn out page after page. Now there are only so many pages a man, any man, can turn out in two hours, but I was sure I broke the record. Afterward, she drove me to Dulles International, which was really sweet because that little honey looked tired.

On the plane I slept deeply; I always do on planes. Something about the movement, the hum of the engines relaxes me. But something about Strawberry's movement had relaxed me, too.

CHAPTER III

I have logged more hours than most pilots; I enjoy flying. The next day, two hours out of Belgrade watching the French landscape near Paris slide by forty-thousand feet below, I could not have felt better. I had just finished a great meal, almost equal to the one I missed at Sans Souci. After the last of the Château Lafite 1974, a great Bordeaux, but a modest vintage so the accountants wouldn't raise eyebrows, I smoked my last cigarette and checked my passport.

I was traveling as a Belgian businessman, French-speaking, though I speak Flemish well enough. I like traveling on a Belgian passport. Everyone has heard of Belgium, and nobody has anything against it. Some of the most troublesome people in the world—police, border guards, customs officials—aren't exactly sure where it is. My cover was that of a textile importer looking into possible deals with Yugoslav mills. It gave me an excuse to be almost anywhere in the country.

Yugoslavia is a country of mountains, rugged highlands, and spectacular coasts. There are fifteen different ethnic groups, all of them industrious and intelligent, but they have also been killing each other off for the last two thousand years. Balkan nationalism makes the Hatfields and McCoys sound like a do-gooder's bedtime story.

Serbs and Croats are the two largest ethnic groups. Both speak the same language, but the Serbs call it Serbo-Croatian and use the Cyrillic alphabet, while the Croats call it Croat-Serbian and use the Roman script. They can't even agree what to call their language or what alphabet to use. Most of the other thirteen groups hate the language, whatever it's called, however it's written.

They were still murdering each other even after the Nazis and Italians invaded and occupied their country. They spent more time killing each other than they did occupiers—except the Fox. But the tension was still there. The KGB and their Stalinist allies CRML in Yugoslavia knew it, and when the Fox went, they'd use it to try and pull the country apart.

There was another aspect to the problem. The Fox got rid of Stalin's boys in 1948, years before old Krush eased them out in the Soviet Union. And he wasn't gentle in the way he did it. The Fox out-Stalined Stalin. But according to Ankevic and others, Stalin's boys just went underground and regrouped, where they remained waiting, still dreaming Uncle Joe's dreams. Everything set them off: dissidents, detente . . . they had been pushing for years to nuke the Red Chinese. Yugoslavia could have been their magic play. A big victory there and maybe they could get back in power in the Soviet Union. It wouldn't be easy. These guys had killed a few million of their own loyal citizens. Your average Russkie, even if he was a dedicated Commie, was not anxious to have them back in power.

I never understood why the big boys didn't put together a deal and cut them off. If the diplomats didn't work things out, sooner or later the hot water would boil over. Anyway, until they got around to it, there would be a lot of extra work for AXE.

It's easy for me to sit back after a meal, smoke my cigarette, and mull things over like a Belgian businessman whose most fearful expectation in Yugoslavia might be a case of indigestion. But the younger guys can't seem to do it. They can't enjoy life, can't sit back, relax, and be Killmasters too. It's never been a problem for me. It's not that I don't see danger coming, but my attitude is different, like that of the men who make a living running whitewater rapids. One of them summed it up for me. He said, "I watch for it. I'm always respectful and I don't move a muscle until the first wave slams into the boat." Now as we approached Belgrade, I could almost see death coming, dancing like a black bull in a field of red tulips.

From the air Belgrade looked as pretty as I'd remembered, almost serene in the white afternoon light. Belgrade means "white city" in Serbo-Croatian, and from the air that day it looked positively glistening. You would never know it was a capital in crisis. No evidence remained that one day during World War II, in a single raid, German bombers killed twenty-five thousand people before lunch.

Belgrade is a lovely city of broad avenues and tree-lined streets, nineteenth-century architecture and color—but the airport is modern, white, and cavernous. And Yugoslavia is a colorful country. People dress in bright colors, not your usual Commie drab.

I was only mildly disguised, a little gray in the

hair, a small mustache tinged with more gray. The suit was Belgian, and so was the luggage. I was surprised when I walked into the terminal and found the place filled with guards with carbines instead of the usual relaxed security. For a minute I thought they had discovered my cover, but I took my place in the custom lines without incident. It soon became clear they weren't looking for me in particular. Yet I could sense someone behind this. Sending OZNA my name and occupation would be too simple. Besides, a simple tipoff might be traced back to them. Hawk would like nothing better than to catch them pulling that one. If I knew him, he would already be setting traps for the Company before I had left D.C. No, whatever had been leaked was ambiguous and indirect. It would be designed to result in my "accidental" capture.

I examined the customs men as carefully as I could. I was looking for telltale signs. Unfortunately I found them. Not one had a pot belly, and their eyes were wrong. The eyes should have been dull and worn out from a life spent going through other people's underwear. These men were sharp, alert. I noticed the bulging biceps under the uniforms. I had an OZNA problem.

They might have a Killmaster problem. Then again, they might not—this was a lousy place for a match. The guards with carbines were some distance away—for carbines an effective distance. The nearest guard was a supervisor with a pistol on his belt, sitting at a desk twenty feet behind the checkers. A long way. Even so, I only had a pistol and they had carbines. The more I added it up the worse it looked. I did have Hugo. But Hugo meant hostages, which doesn't work in Communist countries like it does in the USA. Your hostage gets a medal but he also dies.

They might not have found Wilhelmina, but I had to make a judgement. My judgement was that they would find her. If I waited my turn to see if my judgement was right, I'd be standing right where the system was designed to be most effective—dealing with someone like me. There is an old trick. Most agents don't like using it because it concludes in a violent finale for somebody—although it's not always clear who.

I decided not to wait. I stood as straight as I could. I'm tall anyway. And I marched up to the nearest customs inspector as authoritatively as I could.

I tried standing closer to him than he'd be cozy with. I also tried to stand over him, which wasn't easy. Yugoslavs run big. "UBNA," I said in my best Serbo-Croatian. "Let's go." UBNA was the new official name for OZNA, which supposedly had reformed itself. Party officials and grade-A morons use it, but no one else.

"Let's go to the office," I said. He looked at me completely confused. "Come on," I said harshly. "Do you want me to stand on the customs line like a tourist?" The other customs men looked at me in amazement. Someone pushed a button. I didn't see it pushed, of course, but two big goons suddenly appeared from nowhere. They engaged in a bit of chitchat with the customs men. They didn't necessarily believe I was OZNA, but they didn't know who I was. Yugoslavia is an authoritarian country even if a relatively mild one. They didn't ask questions. If this was some joke, they'd settle with me later the hard way. Clearly, I was a problem for some higher-up to figure out.

While they were still getting their act together I tossed one goon my suitcase and shoved my passport into the other's hand as snappily as I could. Then we started off, a goon on either side. Before we crossed the big room we picked up two more, one in front, one in back. The guy behind me was a monster; I threw him my carry-on bag. He caught it in both hands and whisked it away. He wasn't exactly strong on the brains side. We trooped across the customs area with carbined guards eyeing us, to an innocuous-looking corridor. We turned down the hallway. A uniformed guard was sitting at a high desk a few feet down the corridor, just far enough out of sight so he wouldn't be seen by tourists going through customs. OZNA's lair. The OZNA men visibly relaxed; this was their turf. The hallway turned sharply. We walked past a dozen closed doors. They seemed to be taking me to a gray one at the end of the corridor. They were certainly suspicious of me, but the last thing they suspected was an attack.

In my business, you learn that the element of surprise is sixty percent of success. Not one of them was going to make it to that doorway. Going one on four required a bit of strategy as well as brawn. Lefty moved well but was smaller than the others; he was the first target. Fronty was last; the way I figured it, it would take him some time to turn around. I kicked sideways, straight into Lefty's knee. While I was tilted to my right side in the kick position, I reached down, around my suitcase, which Righty was carrying in his left hand, grabbed his ankle, and lifted, dumping him head first into the wall.

I glanced at Lefty. He was where I thought he would be, down on one knee—but far from out. I brought my right arm across my body to the left, then swung my elbow back into his ear as hard as I could. There was a reassuring pop. The guy on my right was scrambling to his feet. He should at least have been stunned.

Either I had got the angle wrong or Yugoslav walls are substandard for head-knocking. Fronty had turned to face me. Suddenly I was in trouble. As they say in the Marines, I reprioritized my targets. Righty got a roundhouse kick to the side of his head as I turned to face Fronty. I saw Righty's neck jerk but didn't have time to watch the lights go out for him. Fronty was in fighting position— fists up, feet spread wide. I watched his eyes and pushed four or five straight karate punches at him quick as I could. I didn't expect to connect with anything important, and I didn't. But it got him into position. I threw a punch with my right, high and outside. I brought the arm sideways to just the right spot on the side of his head.

Lefty, the tough little bastard, was trying to lift himself up. And there was Backy! He was lumbering at me, swinging a piece of my luggage one goon had dropped, but I was turned wrong. He swung the luggage. I ducked and turned on my left foot. I pushed my right foot into Lefty's face as I went by but not hard enough to do much damage because I had to keep my balance.

It was easy enough to duck Backy's swing, but my balance was such that, standing only on my left foot and still turning, there wasn't much I could do in the way of offense except push until I got my balance back. There was a lot of Backy to push, so

I pretty much wasted my time. I knew he wouldn't be doing anything intelligent with his hands, so I made an awful grimace at him and waved my arms. The poor bastard looked startled. I threw a punch at his face, which of course the stupid bastard blocked with terrific efficiency. Then I kicked him in the groin with my left foot. His whole face twisted up, his eyes crossed, his mind started sliding to the floor. His body followed, doubling over. I interlaced my fingers and brought both hands down behind his neck by way of encouragement. The big bozo hit the floor like a turned-over jukebox. I hoped he wasn't planning to have kids.

No sooner was Backy down when I felt a pain in my right side just below the ribs. I was almost pushed off my feet. Lefty had hit me with a karate chop before he even got to his feet. It hurt. It was the first blow any of them had managed to land. I began to wonder how good a fighter Lefty was; the little bastard was tough, that was for sure. It was hard to tell exactly how tough, though, since he'd been taken off guard. I gave him a kick with my right foot. I aimed for his head, but he blocked it with a raised arm. He didn't see the left foot coming, roundhouse and instep first across the bridge of his nose, until it was too late.

He dropped to all fours, he was hurting. But he lunged for me one more time. I had him. The kick was as hard as I could deliver. I placed it at the base of his skull and used my right foot. He was gone. I wondered for a moment whether Lefty would see morning light. But I looked again, and his neck just seemed to be broken. That was okay by me. I'd just as soon not have a guy like Lefty up and around while I was visiting Yugoslavia.

I picked up my passport, brushed off my suit, and straightened my tie; then I gathered my luggage. Luggage in hand, I walked back the way I had come. The guard was still at his desk. I guess he hadn't heard anything over the din of the terminal. I gave him my twenty-dollar smile, walked up, and socked him behind the temple.

It's certain death to run in a situation like this. I hadn't used Hugo for the same reason. Hugo is quick and deadly, but there would have been buckets of blood and the time saved using him would have been lost cleaning up before I left the terminal. You can't walk by a bunch of guys with carbines when you're covered with blood. You can kill with a stiletto so there is only a drop of blood, but you can't do it with four guys.

I sauntered into the main part of the terminal and headed for the exit, taking my time. I say sauntered, but I sauntered with restraint—showing off can be a dangerous habit.

I had reservations for the Metropol, Belgrade's magnificent old hotel. Now I couldn't go there. It was too much of a risk. The sunlight splashed in my eyes as I walked out of the terminal and hailed a taxi. I gave him the address of a small hotel with no doorman. There was a telephone booth across from it. I would call the special number Hawk had given me from there. I wondered if the safe-house keeper I'd be calling would be as beautiful as the last one I'd stayed with.

CHAPTER IV

As the taxi honked its way through the congested streets, I leaned back and watched Belgrade slide by. I didn't make conversation, I wanted to be as forgettable as possible. But it's not easy. Experience has shown me I'm not a forgettable guy.

Yugoslavia doesn't look like your average Communist country. Not only do the people dress brightly and seem affluent, but they actually look happy.

Belgrade was as bustling as I had remembered, but I noticed a certain melancholy in the air. I didn't realize what it was until the driver turned up his radio to listen to the hourly bulletin on the Fox's health. Suddenly, I noticed the people in the streets standing clustered around anyone with a radio. When the announcement ended, people scattered again, without speaking, just giving each other a nod before going about their business.

We arrived at the hotel with an unnecessary screech. I was thrown toward the front of the car. The driver turned around and gave me a friendly grin, so I just handed him his money. He looked downcast when I gave him Yugoslav notes. Most of the drivers who operate out of the airport report to OZNA, but they like hard currency anyway. They have to fink to keep their jobs, but most could care less. The system isn't really efficient. Still, I waited until he pulled away to walk over to the phone. I called the safe-house keeper.

I didn't know much about her. She wasn't the usual manager but one of Hawk's specials. She was supposed to be able to handle "emergencies," if you know what I mean.

"Hello, Rosa, this is cousin Dmitri," I said, using a Serbian dialect.

"Yes, Dmitri, how are you?"

"Fine, fine. I just got in from Sarajevo." That meant I needed a place to stay.

"Good, you're coming over."

"I had hotel reservations but . . . " Now she knew something had happened.

"No, no, you must come. I was going to the country but . . ." She was asking if I wanted her to go. She sounded sweet, and I was feeling lonely. I thought about it, but what I said was, "No, go ahead and don't stay on my account." She gave me a number where she could be reached, and I said, "Give my love to your mother." It was the affirmation code. "Father" would have meant the exact opposite.

I hailed another cab and was let off at a huge concrete housing project. I suppose it was chosen for the anonymity it offered, but I also thought it offered a good dose of galloping alienation. When the Commies get around to building something it's even worse than the stuff in the West. The paint was already peeling off what seemed like a fairly new building.

The key was under a pretty little woven

doormat. The apartment was bright and cheery in a feminine sort of way—white walls, bright curtains, macramé hangings, pieces of Yugoslav folk art set about. I looked around carefully, checked the closet and drawers; sometimes a safe house becomes unsafe. What I did find was that she was a well-proportioned lady; I could tell from the clothes and the lingerie.

I plopped my luggage on the big bed, threw off my clothes and took a shower. I dried myself and unpacked Wilhelmina and put her together. Then I got the holster from its hiding place in the base of the suitcase. I know a guy who died because he went through Soviet customs with a beautifully disguised pistol and holster stuck between some underwear. I checked Wilhelmina as carefully as a sky diver checks his parachute—my life depends on her. In a few minutes she was in her holster, ready for a ride.

I was tired. I could feel it coming over me. I leaned back on Rosa's white chenille bedspread planning some sweet dreams, but I had to get up and double-check the door. Rosa turned out to have good locks. Then, this naked Killmaster got forty winks. I dreamed about the missing Rosa and remembered the girl in Nairobi whose very long legs seemed to pour from her like a magic waterfall. She had been like the beginning of time—dark, hot, endlessly moving.

He had left her a mess. I guess he wanted that information about me badly. It was a slow, sloppy kill. That, I can't forgive. It is the kind of kill that makes even a Killmaster wake up from his dreams and sit bolt upright. But there was no one to be angry with. Wilhelmina had found her way into his heart when his .38 slug found its way into my shoulder.

My shoulder ached when I woke up. I guess I had been sleeping wrong. I dressed and thought about the dangerous, sloppy meeting coming up. They were amateurs, that was for sure. An open-air café. Amateurs love to meet at open-air cafés. I don't know why. Maybe they think they can outrun bullets. I've seen so many men die in open-air cafés it's like passing a cemetery every time I see one. I like dark, crowded basement restaurants with several exits. With a gun, or even better, a small bomb, you can cause real chaos, enough to actually cover an escape. Besides, unless your opposition is expertly trained they are going to shoot badly in the dark.

I walked there at about three o'clock. The restaurant itself didn't look half bad—wrought-iron tables, folded pink umbrellas. Maybe Ankevic picked this place because it looked pretty. There were ten tables outside, about the right number to give you some cover and still let you keep track of the other patrons. The bay-windowed building across the street was something else again. It looked like it was designed by a moonlighting sniper.

The table I wanted was taken by an old man and a girl. I liked the one set back, where the street opened up into a square. There was a little bit of awning over it, and I liked being only three feet from the corner of the building. I decided to have a look around. The buildings were old, eighteenth and nineteenth century from the look of them. The streets were still cobblestoned. There are few old buildings in Belgrade; the city has been destroyed so many times. I walked out into the square. It felt almost like Venice, except newer. The great old buildings around the square with their fancy Victorian balconies and elaborate grillwork looked like they were built by a different class of people from those who presently occupy Yugoslavia. I suppose in a way that's true. The aristocrats and wealthy bourgeoisie who once lived here might still be doing so if they had been less greedy and a little more patriotic.

When I returned, the old man and girl were still seated at the table. I couldn't tell whether they were lovers or father and daughter, but whatever they were, they were about to leave. I saw the waiter bring the check over. I walked across the street to the tiny newsstand near the corner. I noticed a few out-of-date issues of *Sports Illustrated* and then I bought the Belgrade and Zagreb papers, one in the Roman alphabet, the other in Cyrillic. The couple got up from the table. I paused a minute, then walked over and sat down.

I spread the papers in front of me. The waiter appeared quickly, acting as professional as he looked in black pants and white shirt. I ordered coffee and pastry and looked over the papers. Suddenly, I noticed the bay windows across the street. Very bad. If someone had wanted to set me up for a shoot they couldn't have picked a better spot. Had I been dealing with professionals I would have known immediately what this location meant and aborted the meeting on sight. As it was I just didn't know. I had to play this one out.

The coffee and pastry tasted good, but the longer I waited the more I got worried. Fifteen minutes late. When I get worried, I get watchful, and as my fellow café sitters seemed harmless I concentrated on the passersby.

I watched the eyes and the strides. Appearances are so completely deceiving. It has become trite to get blown away by a harmless-looking little old lady. There are three kinds of eyes that really look at the world: tourist eyes, innocent and excited as a child's; poet's eyes, drinking in everything; and cops' or hunters' eyes. Thieves have them too, and CIA, KGB, and AXE men. As for the rest, most people never look at the world, and you can see that in their eyes, too. Like a cat following a sparrow, I try to spot the watchful eyes before they spot me.

I glanced at my watch. Ankevic was now a half an hour late. I would have broken off the rendezvous, but that meant starting everything from the ground up. So I continued to watch the pedestrians. Forty-five minutes passed and Ankevic had still not shown. My feelings about the meeting had turned totally sour. Then something happened.

The first time she walked by she stood out, but I didn't realize why. She was beautiful—long, blond hair, shapely legs, and all the rest—but a dozen beautiful women had passed by. She kept walking. Five minutes later she was back. Then I realized why I noticed her: she had the wrong kind of eyes. She was very nervous, but she stopped and looked around.

I shifted my weight. I liked the tug of Wilhelmina under my armpit. I slipped my foot over against the base of the table so I could give it a flying push if necessary. I noticed the American couple to my right. If the lead started to fly, they would eat more than their sliced cucumbers. The blond girl examined everyone at the tables, then turned and bolted off. Whoever she was, she was damned obvious. I got ready. You'd have to be a professional to understand why I had gotten so fatalistic, so quickly. I liked being alive. I unbuttoned my jacket—strictly unprofessional—but it would be a little quicker.

She came by again, looking even more serious. I stared at her and when she just looked at me blankly, I motioned her over with my eyes. What the hell, I had nothing to lose.

She hurried over, clutching her purse, her breasts bobbing gently, her three-inch heels clicking on the cobblestones.

"Don't I know you from Skopje?" she said in Serbo-Croatian. It was the code.

"I'm from Zagreb, but I lived in Skopje for five years," I replied.

We went through the rest of it, all of it sounding particularly ridiculous as a way to start a conversation with a woman. Just as she sat down, so delicately on the edge of the chair that you would have thought she had just been spanked, the waiter sprinted over with the menu. She glanced at it quickly and ordered a whole meal. I decided to do the same and ordered a dinner, too. We made chitchat until the waiter walked away. After he left, she kept on talking nonsense. Incredible! She was going to talk about the weather at a rendezvous. Her fluster was beginning to turn to snootiness, so I decided to bring the conversation to a higher plane.

"Who are you?" I asked.

"His daughter, of course."

"Katrina? You don't look like your photograph."

"The picture has the wrong face," she said, giving me a big smile.

"Your name Ankevic is odd for a Yugoslav."

"My father's father was of Greek extraction, but our family has lived in Yugoslavia many generations." I went through her file in my mind and switched to Macedonian, then Slovak, both of which she was supposed to speak and, it turned out, she did.

"Where is your father?" I asked.

"Ah, so now you believe me! You're the Western technician my father sent for?" she whispered loudly in English.

"Speak Serbo-Croatian," I said. "Only lovers can whisper without attracting attention."

"I don't know why my father wanted you, a Jesse James," she said in English. The American couple a few feet away pricked up their ears. I looked up at the windows.

Since she was possibly the last woman I would ever see, I decided to take a closer look at her face. She was more extraordinary-looking than I had first noticed. The blond hair, of course, but she had beautiful green eyes and cheekbones as high as an Indian's. She was also a healthy-sized lady.

There was a tiny scar on the right side of her nose. Most men would have looked at that face for a week and not noticed it. A tomboy accident? I didn't ask, of course. She was beautiful and she didn't like me.

"We don't need you, Jesse James. Why don't you go back where you came from?" she said. I took all this quietly, but she was beginning to annoy me.

"Would your father have asked for our help if he

didn't need it?" I said. "I'm risking my life coming here. It's a serious matter." I didn't tell her I'd risked my life about ten thousand times before.

"We don't need a Western technician. You're scared. Have you got a gun? I want to see your gun. I want to see your gun right now," she demanded in English. I would have dearly loved to slap her across her beautiful face, but I don't hit women.

"You're acting like a spoiled child. Would your father be proud of this performance? There is an American couple sitting right over there," I said in Serbo-Croatian.

"Maybe I'd better go," she said in Serbo-Croatian. I could tell by the way she said it, that she had said this many times, to many men.

I didn't budge. I wouldn't break off the meeting myself, but if she was determined to abort it, there wasn't much I could do.

She started to stand, but then sat back down. Now we both knew each other's limits. She was willing to drive me off but unwilling to take the blame for breaking off the meeting herself.

"When do I see your father?" I asked.

"You don't."

"Are you trying to abort this meeting? Is that what you want? More importantly, is that what your father wants? If so, why are you here at all?" I figured I'd nail her with the last point.

"You won't see my father. He is in the hospital. Intensive care. He was hit by a truck last night, Mr. Jesse James."

"Can he speak?"

"He is in critical condition."

"Maybe we better go." I started to motion the waiter over.

"No, eat your lunch, Jesse James, my tail is covered good," she said in English.

"Your tail is covered very prettily, honey, but I think you mean your trail is covered. I hope you've done that better than everything else I've seen you do or we're both dead."

"Don't be afraid, Mr. Jesse James. I'll protect you from OZNA, even if you *are* afraid to show me your gun."

"You make jokes about OZNA after what they did to your mother and your father? You are playing a child's game," I said in mock disgust. Actually, I liked the fact she could joke about OZNA. It showed the lady had guts. She probably had a little automatic in her purse she figured she could hold off a whole army with.

"We believe in free speech and democracy, like your father. That's why he asked for us," I said. I didn't tell her, of course, that the Company had tried to kill her father at least twice, once in the Fifties in order to discredit the Fox, and once in the Sixties when he opposed us on Vietnam and cost us a lot of liberal support.

She looked dazed. The thing about her father was beginning to get to her. I said: "If you think what happened to your father was an accident, you're wrong."

It started around the eyes. The muscles began to tighten, then tears. She was crying. I motioned the waiter over and looked at him for understanding. The big tip helped to bring it to his face. I scooped her up and off we headed. We got about halfway across the square when she started sobbing loudly. I handed her my handkerchief. It was time to ask some questions.

"Is your father conscious? Can he talk?"

"Sometimes. He gets lost. He forgets what is happening. Mostly he sleeps . . . I'm afraid he is dying."

"How closely is he guarded?"

"Very closely. You'll never get in to see him."

"By the police? OZNA?"

"OZNA, maybe, what does it matter?"

"It matters a lot, to your father. Maybe we can get him out."

"No, no, you don't understand. He works with the Fox now." I took in my breath at this one. Hawk had it figured right. That's why I like working for the man.

"They killed him, they finally killed him, after all these years," she said. She was starting to break down again. I had to stop her. We needed to get as inconspicuous as possible. I put my arm around her.

"Easy, honey," I said. "He's not dead yet. Your old man is as tough as nails, you know that. Prison couldn't kill him." I held her for a while as we walked. "Do you know why he asked for us? Did he ask you to carry on his project?" I asked as delicately as I could, but she remained silent. "I think he needed our help very badly," I went on.

"Where are we going?" she said at last. "I have a place."

"You understand if they hit your father, you shouldn't go back to your apartment."

"No, no I'm not an idiot. We can go to my friends. Don't be afraid, Jesse James. You'll be safe. OZNA would trade you for one of the Fox's boys.

I decided to let that one pass. We began the

usual procedures to eliminate being followed. She was, surprisingly, very good at it. I asked her how so and she said, "All this nonsense—that's why I was late. We have lived with OZNA a long time." I thought maybe I'd underestimated her, but I wasn't sure. I had never seen anything more unprofessional in my life than that little scene at the restaurant.

"I live in Zagreb most of the year. This apartment is someone's that I don't think they are aware I know of."

"Good," I said, doubtfully.

Finally we came to a central hill in the old section of town. Old buildings everywhere but no fancy neighborhood this. It was a slum when it was built in the nineteenth century—tenements and industrial buildings.

"What do you do in Zagreb?" I asked.

"Dance, I design dances. I'm a choreographer."

"Ballet?"

"No, I don't have the build for it." She looked down at her big breasts. "Folk dances."

"I like folk dances," I lied. "Maybe I've seen your group."

"Zagreb Folk Ensemble."

"No, I can't say that I have." I told her about one or two groups I liked a lot. Actually, I'd only read about them.

"Are you of Yugoslav extraction?"

"No," I said, pleased that my Serbo-Croatian might have had her fooled.

"Here we are," she said. It was an old building, maybe turn of the century. It was very dark. The ancient marble stairs were worn by too many feet. The walls were missing chunks of plaster. We walked up four flights—there was no elevator.

"Nice place," I said uneasily.

"There are many artist studios here. It's only one more flight," she said. The landing was lit by a single tiny yellow light bulb that couldn't have been more than fifteen watts. There was a white powder on the floor.

"Marble dust," she said, when I looked down at it. "He is a sculptor."

"Oh."

She put the key in the door and turned the lock. She started to open the door but stopped. "Wait," she said. "Something is wrong." Wilhelmina was in my hand. I edged over to the door and nudged it open with the gun.

"Good night, Mr. Jesse James," she said suddenly. And all my lights went out.

CHAPTER V

I lay sprawled on the floor with a terrible pain in the back of my neck. It occurred to me that I had forgotten something important about Katrina; she was very much her father's daughter. And while the Fox was the toughest and cleverest around, Katrina's father would be a good bet for second place. I should have thought of this a little sooner. My neck and head still hurt, but after a minute or two my vision began to clear. I lifted my head a couple of aching inches and looked around. I was lying on the bare wooden floor of a large white room. I could hear furniture being moved somewhere off on my right. Katrina was sitting on a brown table about twelve feet directly in front of me dangling her beautiful long legs over the edge provocatively. I could have gotten a hard feeling just looking where I was looking, but it wouldn't have been an appropriate response under the circumstances.

She was holding Wilhelmina in her hand and looking down the barrel.

"It's a 9mm. Very nasty," she said to the unseen furniture mover. She noticed I was awake and moved the gun so it pointed at me.

"Well, Mr. Jesse James, are we waking up?"

I didn't say anything. A huge, beefy man wearing splattered sweatpants and sweatshirt came into view. He made some final adjustments to the furniture that had been moved against the walls, then looked around at me. I decided they were planning to torture me. But my would-be torturer had dark, kind eyes.

There are not many kindly-eyed torturers in this world. Their profession marks them as clearly as Cain for the suffering they inflict on their fellow beings. It didn't make sense.

I looked at the beautiful woman sitting on the table and I was sure she was Ankevic's daughter. Despite what I had told her, she looked exactly like her photographs. You can make a mistake from a single photograph but not from three or four. AXE never uses only a single photograph for identification purposes unless it can't be helped. I ran through a checklist. She had known the code. She had known obscure information about the Greek origin of her last name. She knew the languages she was supposed to know. And she was certainly a chip off the old block.

I shifted my position ever so slightly. It told me what I wanted to know. Not only did I have Waldo and Pierre, but Hugo was still in his sheath. If I made the right moves, with Hugo's help, they were both dead. But that didn't make any sense. I couldn't believe she had gone over to OZNA or Uncle Joe's boys after what they had done to her family. I decided to wait until I understood the situation better before I acted.

"So we need the help of a great Western technician, huh?" she said. "Okay, Mr. Jesse James, here is the deal. My father asked for you, but now he is incapacitated and I must take over for him. I don't want you. We have enough goons and secret police in our country already. Yes? But I won't disobey my father's order, so we compromise. If you beat Ivo, maybe you can stay. If you lose, then I have proved we don't need you and I am free to disregard my father's order."

I craned my neck for a better look at Ivo. The guy looked like a sumo wrestler. The furniture had been moved back against the walls so nobody would get injured. It was kind of cute. They thought the contest was going to be like a boxing match. Liberals! I wondered how they had survived all these years. Did they really believe Uncle Joe's boys or the KGB or OZNA would jump in the ring with them and play by Marquess of Queensbury rules? I slid my arms closer to my body and pushed myself up, keeping my eyes on them both. I moved around a bit, loosening up and regaining my balance. I wondered whether to pull out Hugo then and there or wait until the contest was over. I decided it would make a better impression to give a little demonstration beforehand.

"You're an amateur, honey," I growled. "You've just gotten both you and Chubby over there killed." With a flick of my wrist, Hugo was in my hand. With another flick the knife was quivering in the table next to her leg. I said: "At this point, you're dead. I now take three steps forward to your corpse and take the gun from your hand. Bam! Now Chubby is dead." I gave her my finest grin and rested my case.

She stared at me and then pointed Wilhelmina directly at my gut.

"Anybody can make a mistake," she said. She pulled the trigger, but the moment before, she jerked the gun to the right. I had seen it coming in her eyes, and I jumped left. If I had jumped right I would have taken a slug from my own gun. I picked myself up off the floor. As I said, she was an absolute chip off the old block.

"Okay, Mr. Jesse James, now that we have settled that, why don't you have a try at Ivo?"

I looked at Chubby out of the corner of my eye. I figured he was well on his way to being three-minute hash. I shifted to face Chubby. He certainly was built like a sumo wrestler. He watched me carefully. I could tell he wasn't going to make the first move. His gaze was steady, and he kept his center of gravity low, which should have rung an alarm bell for me. I decided to have a shot at him.

I circled around him slow and easy, watching him adjust his position and looking for that almost imperceptible sign that he had shifted off balance even for a moment. I wasn't looking for a big error on his part. I figured just a tiny misstep would do the trick. It appeared to come sooner than I expected. I moved in, hoping to grab his wrist and set him up for a throw. Instead he grabbed mine. The next thing I knew, I was hitting the floor like a ton of bricks.

He had thrown me at a nice, painful angle on the ummatted wooden floor. I must admit I was shaken, but I twisted away from his grasp and spiraled up to face him.

I watched his eyes as we circled around each other. I feinted with a left kick high to his midsection, then feinted again with my right arm. My real shot after these preliminaries was a left uppercut. I expected it to be partially blocked so I brought it up hard as I could. It was a mistake. I landed on the floor again, but this time he kept hold of my wrist. I twisted my arm first in one direction and then another, hoping to convince him that I could twist free that way. Then I swung my right hand out, reaching for a leg. He flipped me over on my side and dragged me across the floor to keep me from getting my balance. I knew he would have to stop moving if he wanted to come down and finish me.

I had been fighting slow and lazy, but suddenly I felt strong and fast. Using his arm as leverage, I swung my feet around and slammed them against his leg while I twisted. I grabbed his wrist and pulled. Damn, I thought, he should come down. He didn't. Instead I hung there like a string on a bow. I was in more trouble now than before. I pushed myself into him, twisting my back toward him and bringing my elbow into his gut as hard as I could. It didn't seem to faze him, so I slammed my heel down on his instep, turned, and tried to twist free. It worked, but I got a nasty blow to the side of my head in the process.

I stood facing him, unsure of what to do next. I felt like I had been fighting in a bowl of Jello. Every one of my moves seemed impossibly slow, but I knew it was an illusion. It was just that from looking at his size and mass, I had trouble accepting how fast he could move. His size and skill made it hard for me to throw him, maybe impossible. I circled him, throwing and pulling some karate combinations. There was nothing behind any of them. I couldn't take any chances he would grab my arm until I caught my breath. I kept circling him looking for an opening. He had great balance and appeared fearless. I kicked to his left knee, low and fast. He moved back quickly. I wasn't doing him any damage, but he also couldn't get a hold on me.

Then he made his first mistake. He glanced at Katrina for a second, just long enough to throw off his defense of my next combination. My right fist came in sideways behind his ear. He felt that one. I let him have a half dozen of my best karate punches. He blocked like a champ, but even blocked they must have hurt. I had the initiative but couldn't keep it. We squared off again. I moved around him kicking hard and low at his legs every time he moved in toward me. It was like fighting a mountain. He was a black belt and a good one. One of us was going to get smashed.

I kept the pressure on his knees and legs, connecting several times. They were conservative kicks by any measure. I was taking as few chances as possible. He reached down and scooped me up by the ankle, anyway. For a moment I hung weightless. Then I came down hard. Chubby moved in to pounce on me, all two hundred and fifty pounds or so. I kicked up at him and rolled, then rolled again. I spiraled to my feet and threw a punch with my right, straight across. He jerked his head back to get out of the way, and I kicked him in the left knee. I ducked and moved around him as quickly as I could, then gave him a side kick into the back of the same knee. I was so busy I didn't see the backhand headed for the bridge of my nose. I dropped to one knee. I was stunned for a moment. I bit my lip viciously and forced myself to my feet, still dazed. I wiped off the blood with my sleeve and kept circling, kicking low to the ankle.

I saw a small, solid-looking chair on one of my turns, only a couple of steps away. I grabbed it and threw it at him hard and high. He caught it in mid-air, laughed, and tossed it back to me. I grabbed it as it went by, crouched low, spinning all the way around with it as fast as I could and let go. This time I was serious. I aimed it low and started moving in to take advantage of any opening it might provide me. He kicked the chair casually aside but in doing so the seat turned and caught him on the knee. I heard him grunt. Since the first toss hadn't been serious he didn't take the second seriously enough.

I kicked high with everything I had. He blocked it with his arm, but was knocked off balance momentarily. I leapt at him and pounded away with both fists, but it was mostly for show. I got what I wanted, though, a hard kick to the same knee I'd been working on. I moved back before those big hands got hold of me, circled right and kicked low, again and again, at his legs.

I hit him solid a half dozen times, but for the life of me I couldn't see he was any worse for it. I backed off, caught my breath, and went in again as committed as a panther. Suddenly he had my arm. I fought to free myself, but the pain was too much. I was forced to the floor, slowly and methodically. If I hadn't gone down, my arm would have broken. But if I had been fighting for my life I might have let him break it first. I saw a foot come down hard next to my head. I pushed and tried to roll. He was getting in position again. The pain was excruciating. I gave him a karate chop across his injured knee. He grunted softly, but I knew this one hurt him. I had been softening up the knee since the fight started. No foot on my head now. He kicked me in the jaw just as I slammed his knee a second time. It felt like a baseball bat when his foot hit me, but I found myself still conscious so I knew it couldn't have been as bad as it felt.

Somehow I had managed to pull away. When I got my bearing I knew it was smash-and-bash time, forget judo, aikido, and the rest. I went for him, intent on finishing him. I felt the adrenalin kick in. I hit him a good one over the right eye. I could see the pain fog him for a second, but he came at me like a charging bull. I popped him a couple of mean ones as I moved out of his way. Then I took a hard one. It looked like a battle of attrition. I moved and hit, and moved, and moved, keeping him off-stride, waiting for a chance to get in something solid. I came in at him fast, trying to catch him out of sync. I guess he was playing the same game on his end, because the next thing I knew, I was taking a sky-diving lesson without a parachute.

I was fast enough and flexible enough that he was never able to follow up on the moves. This time when I slipped loose I kept close to him. I reached for my belt with my right hand. He moved forward. I slashed him across the side of the face with the big brass belt buckle. I swung again for his eyes, but it was a feint. My left foot came in from the other side, smashing into his neck. Then I kicked his weakened knee as hard as I could. He went sprawling on his side. While he tried to get over on his stomach and push himself up, I got in a second kick to his head. I thought it was all over, but I saw him struggling to his feet. I reached for the chair lying on the floor nearby.

"Touch that chair, Mr. Jesse James, and you'll have a second belly button bigger than the first." Katrina had the gun pointed right where she said she did. I looked at her. Out of the corner of my eye I could see Chubby slipping back down to the floor.

"What's that?" she shrieked, noticing the belt in my hand for the first time. I guess she hadn't followed the action. I looked at the bloody belt buckle hanging from my hand.

"What have you done, you son-of-a-bitch? You cheated!" She looked at me with hate and ran over to Chubby. "Ivo, Ivo!" She kept Wilhelmina trained on me. "Move one inch and you're dead." I stayed put. I still had my hand on the chair. She brushed Ivo's hand away from his face and saw the bloody welt.

She looked at me. I had seen that look before. It meant: I am going to kill you.

"Wait," I said. "I did that for a reason. I had Chubby beaten fair and square."

"You're dead," she said. There was a fierce glow in her eyes. She sighted the pistol on my heart.

"I was making a point. Do you think OZNA will play by the rules? You can't fight them with competition judo no matter how good Chubby is."

"That's it for you, Jesse James," she said. I could see her finger curl tighter around the trigger.

"No, Katrina, no," Chubby said as he reached for her arm. "Stop! He is right. Judo is only a sport. I've not been in more than two real fights in my life. Katrina, they won't play by any rules."

She looked down at him and put her left hand on his face. I threw the chair but this time not at Chubby. It knocked Wilhelmina free of her hand. I moved right in after the chair. I grabbed her arm and held it behind her. I was angry: She had been about to kill me until Chubby spoke up.

"How do you think this would have ended if I were OZNA? You just got both you and your friend killed." I tried to fill my voice with disgust. I let her loose and walked over to pick up Wilhelmina. On the way I saw her reach for her jacket pocket.

"Katrina, enough," Ivo said. "This man is a guest in my house. I won't have any more of this." I kept quiet, but she looked at me with eyes full of venom. Ivo put his big arm around her and led her from the room. He had a bad limp.

"He is not a guest. He is a goon," I heard her say as they walked into the hallway.

"Katrina," he said in a calming voice. I went over and pulled out a large overstuffed chair so I could collapse into it. I wasn't feeling too good. My arm felt like it had been burned. I ran my hand along it testing to see if any of the recent repair work had been undone. Everything seemed okay. I took a deep breath and started getting myself together.

Their absence gave me a chance to look around the room for the first time. There actually wasn't much furniture. The large room would still look bare when everything was put back in its place. There were a lot of sculptures around, some made of white marble, others of some kind of black stone. Several were pretty large. I guessed the place was pretty much what Katrina had said it was before she hit me with a sap in the hallway: a sculptor's studio set in the industrial part of town the same way they often are in the U.S. I guess Chubby needed a lot of space to work, plus the big wall-sized windows. I went over to take a look out. There was little traffic and not many pedestrians.

I heard a noise and turned around. It was just Chubby coming in the room, looking sheepish. He had a bottle and three tumblers in his hands. He limped and his face had a bandage on it. Another half-inch and he'd have been a one-eyed sculptor. I was a little surprised to see him up and around. Any one of a dozen blows I had struck him with would have put a normal man out of commission for a week.

He handed me a tumbler and leaned against the table.

"Ivo getting old," he said, continuing in broken English. "Ivo, one-time Yugoslav national champ." He pointed to himself. That made me feel better about having such a hard time with him.

"Sorry about that," I said, pointing to the bandage on his cheek.

"Okay," he said. "Russian vodka, good stuff." He filled my tumbler and then his own.

"Good fighting," he said. We clinked our glasses. He drank it down like water and so did I. He was pleased when he saw my glass empty. He filled us both up again.

"Medicine."

"Medicine," I repeated. We saluted each other and drank it down. Katrina came into the room, gave me an evil look, picked up her pistol, and stalked out. "I don't think she likes me," I said. He said nothing. A minute later he sighed and took a deep breath.

"Move furniture, then more," he said gesturing to the vodka bottle. I helped him move the stuff back in place and almost knocked over a sculpture in the process. I was feeling less pain but more wobbly. When we finished, we both sat down heavily on the couch and drank down another glass.

"Food?" he asked. I shook my head. Food was the last thing I wanted.

"Rest," he said, indicating the couch. He pulled out a brightly colored Yugoslav blanket and laid it on one end.

"Sleep?"

"I speak Serbo-Croatian," I said.

"Okay, good English. American real good." He smiled and waved at me with his hand to lie down.

"Rest," he said and limped off down the hall. I stretched out thinking I'd rest a minute and then think things over. When I opened my eyes, it was eight hours later.

CHAPTER VI

Light filled the room through the large, dirty window. Ivo was sitting a few feet from me in a large, overstuffed chair. I was groggy at first but came around quickly as I always do. The sun was up and it felt warm. As soon as I sat up I realized my body still ached. Ivo reached over with his big hand and gave me a tumbler of vodka.

"Medicine," he said, looking at me sympathetically. I drank it down to be polite.

"Come, we go breakfast. Late now," said Ivo.

"What about Katrina?" I asked.

"Let sleep. Bad day, her father very sick." He continued to speak broken English.

"I speak Serbo-Croatian," I said in that language.

"I know. You said last night. Ivo need practice English. Have forgotten much. Must give speech." His eyes brightened when he remembered his speech.

"Okay," I said, "but not in public. Your speech is about sculpture?"

"Yes, Jesse, about sculpture."

"Nick is the name," I said.

"Okay, Nick. I see." I figured he didn't. Katrina

54

had called me Jesse about twenty times last night, but I let it pass.

"You're sure it's safe to go out? You're not being watched?"

"I'm sure, Nick. Ivo is not political, so why should they watch?"

He gave me a happy smile. What the hell, I thought, and started getting ready.

Once outside it felt good to stretch my legs. We walked a few blocks.

"This area is new," I said.

"Most Belgrade is new, Nick. Bad bombing by Nazis, but even during World War I, much destroyed."

In the cafe we had a typical Yugoslav breakfast of pastry and turkish coffee and talked about innocuous stuff in Serbo-Croatian. He was a fanatical soccer fan like many Yugoslavs. We looked over the papers. They reported the Fox's condition was unchanged.

On the way back I asked him about judo and he told me who he had been up against. He had been matched against the best and had done pretty well. He was strong and well trained, but he just didn't have that driving desire that makes you number one. Ivo had great natural talent, but the bottom line was that he just did not like hurting people.

He showed me around his studio. It was a big room, even larger than the living room, and filled with statues and sculptures, some completed, some mere outlines. There were tools, chisels, mallets, gouges, drills, and barrels of plaster of Paris and ladders scattered around. He did a lot of big stuff. Some of it was larger than he was. Most were of figures that were realistic in their detail but not abstract either.

"Do you know who?" he asked. I'd been standing in front of a large female nude for several minutes. I had just started to tell him no when I realized it was Katrina. She looked twice as good as I had imagined.

At that moment, she wandered into the studio looking for Ivo, I suppose. When she saw me, she walked out without saying anything. I started to ask her how her father was, but she waved me off.

"Very friendly," I said.

"Very unhappy," he replied, getting ready to go to work. I pulled up a chair. He was working on a large marble statue of a seated woman, but Katrina hadn't posed for this one. The model must have weighed almost as much as Ivo himself.

"Why didn't you use a thinner model?" I gave him a wink and made a shape in the air.

"Sometimes," he said, pointing to several statues around the room. "But you know Playboy bunny too easy to make beautiful. Make fat lady beautiful is hard. You understand?"

"Sure," I said. I relaxed and watched him chip away. Those massive arms and hands had a delicate touch when it came to his work. He looked around at me. He was carving something at the foot of the woman. He gave me a big, toothy smile.

"What is?"

I should have known immediately what it was. I had been watching him work on it. I walked over for a closer look. I had watched one ear appear and then another. The rest was barely outlines. It looked like a lump of stone.

"A cat," I said. He laughed and patted me on the back.

"Good, good," he said, continuing to laugh. He was obviously pleased with his creation. It was a wonderful joke to him to be able to carve a cat. I watched him for a few more minutes, but I didn't plan to sit around all day. I went to look for Katrina. She was in the kitchen leaning against a table, eating a piece of bread.

"Hey," I said. "That will stick to your hips."

"What can I do for you, Mr. Jesse James?"

"What's happening?"

"Today, nothing, as far as you are concerned. Tomorrow, maybe something. Rest. Play tourist."

"What about you, what are you doing today?"

"That's for me to know and you not to worry about."

I eyed her for a moment. I had some ideas. "I have to go get my luggage. Maybe I'll take in a couple of art galleries and be back this evening," I said.

"You've seen no sign the apartment is being watched?"

"None."

"Please be careful coming and going. Ivo doesn't know anything about politics or care. I don't want anything to happen to him."

"I can understand that," I said.

I picked up my stuff at the safe house and brought it back over. It was already late afternoon. Katrina was out. Ivo didn't know where, and he was busy working. I took a cab to Belgrade's Frescos Museum, ducked out a side door, and caught another cab to within half a mile of the hospital. I walked the rest of the way. I had decided to drop in for a chat with Katrina's father. After all, it was the old man himself who had asked for me. One thing was certain: Katrina would tell me as little as she could. If I couldn't find out what was happening from Ankevic I'd just have to play along, and that could be dangerous for all of us.

The hospital building looked new. Hospitals look the same around the world, but more importantly, they are a difficult kind of building to make secure. There are so many employees, patients, relatives, rooms, closets, doors, labs—that's what I like best about them. I looked over my sport coat and shirt and walked in with an air of authority. It didn't take me long to borrow a stethoscope and white coat. Suddenly I was Dr. Nick. No one challenged me, and the first part of the operation went smoothly. I was genuinely relaxed.

It took me a while to find out which floor Ankevic was on without drawing attention to my inquiries. Now came the tricky part. They had cordoned off the whole floor he was on. Except for other intensive-care patients and their doctors, no one was admitted. I would have to go up there without any clear idea of the security arrangements. I waylaid a nurse to see if I could learn anything more. I complained loudly that the security measures were interfering with my duties. She told me conspiratorily to be careful, there were OZNA around and why was I bothered anyway, there was no one on that floor but intensive-care patients. I told her I had just had a patient moved up there. She explained what I would have to do to be admitted to the floor.

I had to call the floor, tell them my name and my patient's name, my reason for going up, and wait to be paged. If everything checked out, guards would come and get me and take me up in a special elevator. What I needed now was information. I looked for an out-of-the-way nurses' station. It took me a while to find one. I was going through the files when a nurse supervisor came up and asked if she could help me. She was suspicious and persistent. She wanted to know my name. I gave her my big smile and popped her on the jaw. I dragged her behind the counter and tied her up with her shoelaces and pantyhose, then tucked her into a nearby closet. I wrote a little sign which said "Do Not Open" and pasted it to the door. Then I tried my best to jam the door shut, all the while keeping a weather eye for new company. It came in the form of a young, helpful nurse who walked up just after I had got things tidied up. She showed me where the records I was looking for were.

I put doctor, patient, and disease together and made my call. I waited. There were two armed guards in the elevator when it came down. They looked me over, seemed satisfied, and up we went. I walked out on the floor. The elevator guards remained where they were, but I had to explain to the two guards sitting at a nearby desk who I was.

"You know the way," they said, looking satisfied with my explanations. But of course I didn't. I walked slowly down the hall, eyeing the numerous gunmen. They were carrying Czech-made Skorpion machine pistols—awfully heavy weaponry for guard duty. I walked down the corridor, but I was approaching a bad problem. The intensive-care nurses would know I wasn't Dr. Kosovo. From the small sign high up on the right side of the passageway, I decided the unit would be somewhere around the next corner. I turned the corner, nose in the air. Two guards stood in front of a doorway, looking as tough and well trained as the others. I walked on by, nodding to them as I passed. They didn't respond but instead eyed me coldly. I kept walking until the hallway made another sharp angle.

Finding myself alone in the corridor, I pushed my way into the nearest room. It was a small ward that must have been cleared out for security reasons. I looked around and then went over to the window. I couldn't see much, so I kicked out the screen. I leaned out and looked to the left toward the guarded ward. The building was built sort of like a checkerboard. Only the squares represented by the protruding windows were separated from each other by about three feet. The windows were fitted in what looked like precast concrete squares. In any case, they stuck out about four inches from the rest of the building. I looked straight down. The building consisted of a wide, two-story building from which the narrow ten-story tower I was in emerged. So I was partially protected from anyone seeing me move along the outside of the building. I was on the east side of the building, and it was getting dark and the trees from the park across the street further blocked the view. I looked at my watch and decided to give myself another half hour before making my move.

When the darkness outside was complete, I took a look at the ledges again. I'm an experienced technical climber, so I was only mildly worried. If I had had the proper equipment there would have been no problem at all. I took off my shoes and socks and stuffed them in my coat pockets. Then I took off my white doctor's coat and tied it around my waist. I climbed out on the windowsill. I looked down. The drop was certainly enough to kill me. Climbing along the segments was going to be no problem. There were two concrete ledges on top so I could reach up and place fist jams to hold myself.

Getting across the space between the segments was going to be a little tricky.

I made my way along the first window segment without a problem, although I didn't realize how windy it was until I had gotten completely outside. I reached the end of the segment. The next ledge was three feet away. I jammed my left fist as tight as I could and angled over the gap with my leg. I pushed myself out into space, first balancing on my left foot, then on my right. I did a jam with my right hand and released my left. It wasn't as bad as I figured. I moved across the next segments as quickly as I could. Crossing to the third segment I slipped. I was hanging by one hand for a second but I finally got a firm hold with my other hand. The wind was giving me more trouble. It looked like I had another problem. The next window was lit. After some difficult maneuvers I managed to peek in the window.

I could move up or down; either choice was dangerous. I chose up. To get up there I had to do a stem jam; my back would be against one slab and my feet against the other. Not a hard move if you know how to do it, and if you have a nice deep crevice to ascend. The vertical protruding slabs gave me a little more depth than horizontals, but it still amounted to only about five and one-half inches, which meant I had to use my free left arm in tricky ways that were tricky even when you are as skilled as I am. I made it clambering the last foot. I was sweating like I had been in a sauna. I sauntered along the next segment. Dropping down was not as difficult, though I wouldn't do it as a parlor trick.

I made it the rest of the way across to Ankevic's window without any problems. I peeked in. Two guards sat in the middle of the room with machine pistols in their laps. There was a partition behind them. I assumed that was where Ankevic was. I heard voices and pulled back just in time. A guard walked up to the window, turned slightly, and tossed a bottle into a wastepaper basket. There were at least two more guards I couldn't see. The game was all over. All my effort had been for nothing. I dangled outside the window for another five minutes hoping a miracle would happen. When the time I had allotted myself was up, I scuttled back over ledge after ledge until I came to the lighted window. I didn't want to climb a story again unless I had to, so I took a peek. It was empty now, so I yanked out the screen and pulled myself in.

I had almost crossed the room when the door opened a foot, but the intruder stopped, turned, and began to answer an unseen questioner. By the time he had stopped speaking and turned to come in the room, I was behind the door. I caught him with a karate chop on the back of his neck and pushed the door closed with my foot. If he had come a minute later I would have hidden, but as it was, I just didn't have time. He dropped in my arms. I pulled him over to a nearby corner, pulled open a door that turned out to be a closet, and stuffed him in.

The door began to open again so I ducked in the closet myself. I soon realized they were using the room as a lounge. I couldn't make out what they were saying, but it didn't amount to much at first. Then I realized they were talking about the Fox. They were talking about guarding him. That information did unpleasant things to my brain. These weren't a bunch of OZNA's thugs, they were the

Fox's bodyguard, and they were good. Suffice it to say that over the last forty years nearly every major espionage agency in the world had tried to kill the Fox at least once and he was still alive. It was time for Nick to take a powder.

I knew then I was going to have trouble getting out of the hospital alive. No wonder the bastards were carrying Skorpions.

I waited until the guards finished their coffee and left. I was heading for a window when I heard a familiar voice. Katrina! I hurriedly put on my shoes and rearranged my white coat. Then I opened the door wide and walked out into the hall with a big smile on my face. I could see five guards in the hallway. Katrina was talking to one a few feet away. I walked right over to her.

"Miss Ankevic, I must speak with you a moment." She turned to face me. When she saw who I was, her eyes went wide for a second. I was sure she would scream. In preparation for which I said: "No, Miss Ankevic, your father is still alive." She put her hand to her mouth. I took her arm and walked down the hallway toward the elevators.

"What are you doing here?" she asked angrily in English.

"If you don't speak Serbo-Croatian, I'll have to hurt you," I said with a big, friendly smile.

"You wouldn't last long, Jesse James. These are the Fox's bodyguards."

"So I've gathered. Nice of you to let me know before I came walking in here."

"If you had followed orders and remained in the apartment you wouldn't be in so much trouble. You're supposed to help us. You don't run things, you don't make decisions. I do."

"This is not a good place to discuss our problems. Right now my big objective is getting out of here alive."

"What do you want me to do?"

"Just keep walking with me to the elevators. After I've gone down, ask the guards who I was. Tell them I was a doctor you had never met before."

We waited for the elevator without speaking. I wasn't too worried. I had Wilhelmina in my pocket, and Hugo up my sleeve. I hoped Katrina wouldn't scream and betray me and that we'd be pals from here on out, but I wasn't depending on it. You can't assume such things in my profession.

When the elevator arrived, we shook hands formally and I said: "Your father needed something important done. I hope you are doing it." She flushed, then turned and walked away. I figured I'd leave her with something to think about. But she got herself together very quickly. As she walked down the hallway, she turned around to stare at me. She flashed me a hard look. I had a nice, quick ride downstairs with the two elevator guards. They let me off on the second floor. I stood waiting for the elevator to take me to the first, that was the system. It was a long time coming and I didn't see any stairs. The alarm went off just before the second elevator opened on the first floor.

People stopped and stared around, not knowing what to do. I walked through the bright, crowded lobby. There were a dozen guards at the front door. They were regular police rather than the Fox's bodyguard. Still the odds were bad. I looked around and saw a side exit. There were two uniformed guards standing in front of the double doors. One already had his pistol in his hand, the other was still fumbling around for his. In a minute the Fox's Skorpion-packing guards would be behind me. I wouldn't last long. I walked down the neon corridor toward the doors at a calm, even pace. They pointed their pistols at me.

"Stop!"

"A homicidal maniac is loose," I said. "I am his doctor." I'm not sure they believed me, but they didn't shoot and I kept walking.

"Doctor, you can't leave. Orders."

"I know, I know, you oafs. I'm his doctor and I'm looking for him. Why are you pointing those guns at me? You fools. I've come to tell you what the man looks like."

They let me walk right up to them. I glanced around. Down the corridor I could see two of the Fox's bodyguards headed in our direction. What happened next is one of those things that is bound to occur in my profession, one of the things nobody likes to talk about. The two guards in front of me were a couple of innocents, not OZNA, not bodyguards, not police. They had been handed pistols, promised pensions, and told to guard a hospital.

I flicked my wrist. Does a cobra see its own strike? The one on the right clutched at his fibrilating heart, the young, pimply-faced one on the left tried to stop his throat from gushing blood. I pushed through to the door, wiping Hugo on a shirt sleeve as I went by. Neither man had uttered a word or got off a shot, even though their pistols had been pointed at me. I was running down the steps outside when I heard the first bursts from the Skorpions splattering through the doorway.

Out in the street I melted into the crowd, pulling

off my white coat as I went and tossing it into the garbage can. That was the end of Dr. Nick. I took the usual measures to make certain I wasn't being followed. It took some time, but I was sure that I had gotten away free.

When I arrived back at Ivo's studio, I thought it was deserted, but then I found him in his studio exactly where I had left him hours earlier. There was more cat visible than earlier. He was tapping out cat whiskers and chuckling to himself with pleasure.

"How you like, Nick?"

"Looks like cat whiskers to me," I said.

"Medicine, Nick?"

"Yeah," I said, "why not?" I found the cabinet he told me he kept it in and hunted up a couple of glasses.

"Ivo," I said, "what's this all about? I can't help unless I know what's going on."

"You will have to ask Katrina. She told me not say. Her father is very great man, Nick. He did much protect artists years ago."

"But how can I help if she won't tell me anything? Are you a political dissident like Katrina?"

"Katrina is my friend, Nick. I don't know politics. Her father great man. I make freedom statements in stone." He gestured to his cat.

"How are a cat's whiskers a statement?" I asked. He was bent over finishing them as carefully as if his life depended on how they turned out.

"Is good whiskers, no, Nick?" he said. I laughed. What could I do? I'd get more information out of Katrina.

"More medicine?" I asked, filling the tumblers.

"Okay, Nick," he said.

CHAPTER VII

"Bastard! Son-of-a-bitch!" Katrina had a few more choice words for me in Serbo-Croatian as she pounded on my still half-asleep body. I grabbed her and we rolled around on the floor awhile. There were things I'd much rather have done rolling around on the floor with her other than fight. She smelled and felt great. I pinned her arms to the floor and asked her what she was mad about. She almost spit at me.

"Those two men you killed, you bastard! You didn't have to do that. You shouldn't have been at the hospital. Two people died unnecessarily because of you."

"First of all," I said, "who are you to second guess me about whether or not the guards had to be killed? Have you ever been in a fight? What do you think happens when you get caught in a narrow corridor by a couple of guys with machine pistols?" I gave her a hard stare. "Second. You lied to me. If you had told me the Fox's bodyguard was protecting your father, I never would have gone. And third, you blew the whistle too soon before I had a chance to get out of the building. You're as responsible for those men's deaths as I am." That would give her little liberal heart something to feel guilty about.

"You son-of-a-bitch!" she said, tears welling up in her eyes. "Trying to blame this on me." Ivo chose that minute to wander into the room. Finding us lying pelvis to pelvis, he discreetly walked back out again.

"It's war," I said. "These things always happen in war. Do you really think only the bad guys get killed? Why do you think everybody in their sane mind is for peace?"

"You give me lectures about peace. You're a professional murderer. You've been here two days and already the violence has begun. Those poor men had families."

"The way I figure it you shouldn't carry a gun unless you plan to use it. Do you think they wouldn't have stopped me? I'd be the one who is dead. And I didn't start the violence. Your father wasn't hit by accident."

"You don't know that," she said. I sighed and rolled off, letting her get up.

"You're an animal, do you know that?" she said as she stood.

"It wouldn't have happened if you had told me what was going on."

"Mr. Jesse James, if I don't feel you are going to cooperate and follow orders, I'm not going to take you along no matter how much you might be needed. Do you understand?" She turned and stalked out of the room.

Her last point was a good one. I myself wouldn't involve anyone who I thought was going to come in and try to take over and not follow orders.

I heard pots and pans banging around in the

kitchen, cabinet doors being opened and closed. I leaned back in a chair. There was nothing I could do for the moment.

Ivo walked in after a while and shared a bottle of vodka. He sat on the couch, his bulk so large that he took up almost half of it. "Katrina likes you," he said to me smiling.

"That's not the impression I get," I said, sipping my vodka.

"She is chip off the old block, Nick. She is stubborn like two mules, but she has a good stomach. Her father was in prison. Her mother is dead. Aunts and uncles not the same thing. Yes?"

"Guts," I said. "She has guts. That's how you say it in English." I didn't see any reason not to help him work on his language skills.

"She has good guts," he repeated. I realized then that Ivo was never going to be as good at linguistics as he was at sculpture.

"She won't tell me what is going on," I said. "That makes things very dangerous."

Ivo didn't say much by way of reply, just poured me some more vodka.

Actually finding the Fox's bodyguard protecting Ankevic confirmed Hawk's analysis of the situation down to the fine print. "To" but not "including"—that was my problem. People were going to die because I didn't know the details and couldn't prepare a plan.

Two things were clear. Yugoslavia had to be in a terrible danger or the two men wouldn't have been forced to work together. And the Fox must have figured out some way to use Ankevic to defeat the threat. The first piece of information pointed to the KGB and the local Stalinist CRML cells as the enemy or why else choose Ankevic? But the second piece of information yielded nothing. What could Ankevic and a few dissidents do to stop the plot? I had only Katrina's slip that we would be going somewhere. My musings were interrupted by sounds of an argument from the kitchen. I couldn't follow all of it through the closed door, but I gathered she had set only two places for dinner. A few minutes later I was called in to eat.

Katrina looked a little chastened during the meal. She sat silently, picking at her food and looking thoughtful. The main course was *teleca corba leso*, a rich, spicy stew made with veal, sausage, red and green peppers, and tomatoes. They toss an egg or two in at the last minute which sounds a bit strange but tastes good. We drank a couple of bottles of fine Serbian wine called Negotinsko. We finished off with turkish coffee and dishes of sweet noodles. Ivo was a big eater, I noticed, but a civilized one. We talked mostly about soccer. Ivo planned to take a year off from sculpture to travel around the world and attend soccer games in every city and country he went to. That was the big dream of his life.

I was worried about what would happen to him after we left. I suggested he leave soon, but he told me about how many commissions and sculptures he had to do. I looked to Katrina for help.

"It might be a good time to go, Ivo. Things could become very dangerous here." She looked at him worriedly. "I know they have never harmed you before. You've been protected because you are the most famous sculptor in our country"—Ivo blushed when she said this—"but this might be different. They were afraid to attack my father for

many years after he got out of prison because of all
the books he wrote. They might make it look like
an accident."

"But, Katrina, I'm not political, I don't know
anything. Ivo is not afraid of goons." He flexed his
massive arms.

"I think you should go for a while," I said.

"I'll think about, Nick," he said. But involun-
tarily he glanced back toward his studio and his
unfinished work. I knew he wouldn't leave but said
nothing more. I rested my chin on my hand and
watched Katrina slowly finish her dinner. Ivo got
up saying he had some work to finish in the studio
and left us alone.

"Okay, Mr. Jesse James, I'll tell you where we
are going and why." She still sounded firm, but
something in her had changed. She sounded weary.
Maybe she had realized we were playing for keeps.
Ivo probably had a lot to do with it.

She went on. "You know the Fox drove out the
Red Army and broke with Stalin in 1948. When the
Fox broke with him, Uncle Joe had fifteen thousand armed followers in our country. This is not
counting the Red Army. The Fox had a few of these
Stalinists shot, but most were sent to camps. They
were forced to write confessions and reform themselves. After that, all but a few diehards were released. Almost no one was killed. My father always
believed that the Fox's tactics just drove the
Stalinists underground and that if the Fox had
fought them fairly, they would have collapsed completely because they had no support among the
people.

"Unfortunately for us, my father was right and
only a few weeks ago the Fox learned they were

much stronger than he thought. They have formed an elaborate network of cells and call themselves, in English, the Committee to Return to Marxist-Leninism, CRML. We call them Uncle Joe's fan club and make a joke, but they are serious and very dangerous. They are waiting for the Fox to die to make their move. The secret, the Fox learned, was that they had infiltrated OZNA, the party, and the armed forces.

"My father was shocked when he received the Fox's invitation. At first he refused to go, thinking it was some kind of trick. But they pleaded with him so that he finally consented. He had not spoken to the Fox in thirty years. Remember that at one time he was the Fox's right-hand man and heir apparent. They were personally very close. My father had been worried for some time about CRML and always had his own sources. He believed that the Fox had failed to break them with his purges and indeed thought he had discovered evidence that CRML had infiltrated the Fox's own secret police, OZNA, but his evidence was inconclusive. Still, he was shocked by what the Fox told him. A man they both knew well confessed on his deathbed that he had been blackmailed into working for CRML and in turn for the KGB twenty-five years ago. This man told the Fox there were others being blackmailed, called them the 'controlled ones.' But he did not know who they were. That's how all this began. We have to prove the controlled ones exist, that's where I will need your help."

I took all this in in silence, sipping my coffee. Then I said stoically, "How?"

"There are documents buried in the mountains

that prove the controlled ones exist. All the names are listed there too. We have to go on a long journey."

"Journeys are fine," I said, "but the longer the journey, the easier it is to pick up fellow travelers."

"What do you mean?"

"I mean that for starters I hope you covered your trail tonight when you came back here. From now on, every little mistake we make will carry with it the possibility of being fatal. Mistakes build on top of one another, too." I waited for a response. None came. "Can you tell me if you were followed."

She gave a start. She said she had been careful, but her expression clouded with doubt for a moment.

"Even if they can't follow you—or us—without being obvious, they'll go through lists of everyone you know and stake out each apartment until they find you."

"You are probably right, but I have only stayed here two nights and we leave tomorrow. I've endangered Ivo enough."

"Ivo is not afraid." The sculptor had picked that minute to come back into the room. "Katrina is my friend. I want to help."

"No, I want you to stay out of this. You have your work to do," Katrina said. "Did you get the packs?"

"Oh, yes. I bought them and the rest of what you asked for. I'll get them," he said.

"We had better pack tonight so we will be ready. Ivo will take us to the train station tomorrow."

"Why the train? That seems unnecessarily slow. Why not take a car?"

"Whose car do you have in mind? I can't take mine. We can't take Ivo's or any of his friends' without getting them involved in all this." She threw up her hands.

"We'll steal one."

"Just the sort of suggestion I would expect from you. No. We go by train."

"It doesn't make sense."

"Mr. Jesse James," she said. "We do it my way or not at all. Are you coming or not?"

I nodded. I would go along with her plans for now.

"Please help pack," she said.

We cleared the table and soon it was piled high with food and equipment. Ivo's packs were old-fashioned but serviceable. I checked through the gear.

There was a small, lightweight frying pan, nesting cooking pots, canteens, cups, a coffeepot, spoons, forks, knives. I got a piece of paper and wrote out a list. Mistakes, when you are far away from civilization, are usually serious. Sometimes they make you uncomfortable. Occasionally they make you dead.

Katrina sat across from me bagging up the food. She did not have freeze-dried food like we use in the U.S., so we would have to carry more weight. She brought fresh vegetables, peppers and tomatoes and onions, some cloves of garlic, as well as the dry stuff.

I looked over the clothes. There were sweaters, extra pants, down jackets, a stocking cap and gloves. The big danger in spring is not freezing, but hypothermia. Your heating system gets overloaded and can't cope with the heat loss. It happens when you're tired, hungry, wet, and cold. This combination has killed people even in temperatures of forty or fifty degrees. Wind is the key. If you're wet and can't get dry, you can die in what seems like warm weather.

"My problem is boots and socks," I said to Katrina. "If I'd known we were going mountain climbing I would have brought my own."

"Ivo will get the name and address of a store for you. You can buy some tomorrow."

"We're leaving early, aren't we?"

"Not until tomorrow night. I have to go to the hospital and make the rest of the arrangements."

"I know professionals, Katrina. Every hour we're here is dangerous. The more important you are to them, the quicker they'll locate us."

"Nothing can be done," she said. "Everything is arranged for tomorrow night."

"We should get some basic climbing equipment," I said. "A rope, a couple of caribiners, some pitons, and a rappel sling. We can gct up and down a mountain quicker that way. Have you done any climbing?"

"I haven't, but buy the equipment you think is necessary."

I started packing my stuff. I did it carefully, putting heavy stuff high in the pack and close to my back for balance. Then I went and got my binoculars, my special minicamera, and ammunition for Wilhelmina.

After I got back in the kitchen and started putting stuff away, Katrina said, "I know what you are thinking, Mr. Jesse James. As you say in America, I get this girl off in the woods and get in her pants real easy. I warn you now. I have a pistol. I will shoot you."

I smiled. "The thought never entered my mind.

Rest assured I will not touch you."

"Hey, what is all this bad talk?" said Ivo, coming in the door. "We are friends working together. I don't understand you, Katrina. You used to say make love not war. Now you are always threatening people. Mr. Jesse James is guest in my house."

"He is not a guest or a friend. He is a secret police, a Western OZNA. If they ordered you to kill me and my father, you would do it, wouldn't you?"

"They would never order me to do that," I said uneasily.

"But if they did, you would do it, wouldn't you? You would do anything they ordered you to do, kill anyone they told you to. Ivo, you must understand this is not a human being. This is part of a powerful machine. You point to him and say 'Kill' and he kills."

"Katrina, he is a human being. I don't want you talking about guests in my house like that. All these arguments give Ivo a headache." He got up. "Stop this fighting. There are enough enemies out there." He gestured to the street with his thumb as he walked out of the room.

CHAPTER VIII

I waited for Katrina to get ready to leave for the hospital so that I could follow her. I was sitting up on the windowsill, watching the street.

"You sit in the morning sunlight like a cat, Nick," Ivo said, "but unlike a cat you get more tense instead of relaxed."

"Just thinking things over, Ivo."

"This is very dangerous thing you and Katrina do, yes?"

"That doesn't bother me. I just want the mission to be a success."

"Ivo understand Katrina will be ready in a minute. I think you have the address of the camping store?"

"Yes. Everything is fine." I kept my eyes on the street. Katrina yelled "goodbye" from the door. I watched her from my window perch until she was half a block away and then went down after her. I wanted to make sure no one else was following her.

She was good. It took her about twenty minutes to lose me. Perhaps I worried unnecessarily. Still, following someone is most effective with a team. Even the best individual is not as good a shadow as a trained squad.

I found the camping store without difficulty and bought the climbing rope and other stuff we needed. I picked out the lightest and softest boots they had which would still offer my feet some protection. When I got back I circled Ivo's block, checking to see that the building was still secure. On the way up the stairs to Ivo's studio I noticed a good place to hide the clothes and other valuables I wouldn't be taking with me. I borrowed a chisel and mallet from him and hid my belongings behind the wooden stairs just before the landing. I told Ivo where I'd hidden my things and to burn them if I didn't come back.

"Ivo, you be careful," I said when I returned his tools.

"Sure, Nick. You need help, let Ivo know."

She returned at dusk. I watched her coming through the crowd, her beautiful long legs, her head held high. She was being tailed. I wasn't sure at first, but there was something funny about a small man in a blue suit. He didn't look at her directly, but then there was no reason for him to stop where he did. I put the binoculars up to my eyes and followed his gaze to a green car with three men in it. He began walking again. I watched him until he moved out of sight. There were others now. It took me awhile to pick them out.

Katrina came into the room all smiles. "He is better today," she said happily to no one in particular.

"Mr. Jesse James likes to watch birds," she said when she saw the binoculars in my hand. "Or is there a girl across the way taking a shower?"

"They've found us. You were followed."

Katrina walked up beside me. I handed her the binoculars and pointed out the men. She took the binoculars and watched the street carefully.

"I'm not sure," she said.

"Look at the green car. You can see the guy on the right using the communications equipment."

"I can't believe it. How could they? Look, the green car is leaving."

"The van behind them is their replacement."

"I don't see . . . What are we going to do? I'm not sure about that van of yours, but the man across the street is watching this building."

I took the binoculars, but I didn't really need them. One thing I did notice was that Yugoslav communications equipment was big and bulky compared with American or, for that matter, Soviet. They seemed to have communication only from vehicle to vehicle. Their street operatives had to rely on sight and gesture. That was good news. It would make my job easier.

"How could they . . . ?" she said, puzzled. I didn't say anything.

"Ivo," she yelled. "They have found us. We must go now." Ivo came bursting into the room.

"What can I do, Katrina—I know, you must take my car."

"No! Let me think."

"There'll be more in a few minutes. We must move quickly or there'll be too many for us to escape," I said, trying to hurry things along.

"So what do you suggest, Mr. Jesse James?"

"I'm going to draw them away," I said. "You wait here exactly five minutes after I leave. Meet me at the southeast corner of the square near the train station."

"They'll see your pack and know you're going to the station," she said nervously.

I thought a moment.

"Ivo take packs," the sculptor cut in. "You and Katrina go, the way you plan, Nick. I will meet you at the park."

Katrina looked at me. "Only if you promise to leave the country," she said to him firmly.

Ivo shifted uneasily and looked at his feet. Katrina looked at me again. We both knew he wasn't going to leave.

"Okay, Ivo," I said. "I'll help you put the packs in boxes. Then you can load them into your car. But let's hurry. In a few minutes they'll have enough men out there to follow anyone who comes in or out of the building."

I watched Ivo load the car while Katrina paced the room like a jaguar in a cage.

When Ivo returned I said, "If anyone is following you, Ivo, try to lose them before you reach us. But if you can't, put your headlights on low beam when you come up the road. I'll take care of them."

She started to say something, but I cut her off. "Okay, I'm going." I took one more look out the window before going downstairs. I poked my head out the front door and then followed with the rest of my body. They weren't going to shoot me; they wanted to know where I was going first.

The streets were wet and shiny from the rain and looked eerie in the yellow street lamps, but I didn't have much time to appreciate the view. Four men piled out of one of the cars and stood around for a moment in a huddle. The van remained, along with one more car to play it safe, I figured. I turned right and walked in the opposite direction from my destination, then cut across a broad street to throw them off balance.

We were about six blocks from Ivo's studio and I could still sense them behind me. At one point I made a sharp left turn past a closed cafeteria and noticed there were only three of them. Probably one had stopped to tie his shoe and got lost.

There was no sign of a car following us. I looked at my watch. Katrina would have left already. I had, I figured, about three or four minutes to do the job I had planned and still meet her on time.

Katrina had told me about a cul-de-sac about half a mile from the station, and that's where I headed, moving at a quick but unhurried pace. When I reached it I entered without hesitation. A lot of guys are leery of them because there's only one way out—one easy way, that is—but that doesn't bother me. When I go through the opposition, one way's as easy as another.

The asphalt streets turned to cobblestones as we approached. I felt my heart rate go up, but otherwise I was as solid as a rock.

The street was dark and very slippery. One old man was hobbling along. "OZNA," I said. "Get inside." He scuttled for a doorway. I could hear footsteps clicking softly on the cobblestones behind me. I walked to within thirty feet of the end of the street and stepped into a doorway, making it look as if I were going to visit someone. Out slid Wilhelmina with my back still to them. I leaned out to get a look at my hunters and immediately ducked back. A silent bullet had nicked the door inches from my head. There was another shot, and I saw shadows fan out. Apparently they had lost interest in knowing where I was going.

Just then one of the shadows stepped under a light—a big mistake. From my position in the dark, protected doorway I saw the shadow was a man. I aimed and fired.

While he dropped onto the damp, cold stones and the scent from Wilhelmina was still pungent in the cool night air, another shadow cut across the cul-de-sac. It too fell, this time with a reverberating thud. I watched his gun go sliding across the cobblestones and come to a rest against a door jamb. So far, so good, I thought, swinging Wilhelmina around to seek out the remaining hunter.

He leaned out a bit too far from behind the front of a gray sedan and I shot him in the neck. His whole body lurched forward and then was still. I carefully studied the cul-de-sac, looking especially hard for the fourth hunter, but there was no one else.

The whole thing had lasted maybe thirty seconds. Although the sound of the rain had muffled the shots, along with the silencers, several people were still at their windows. I was gone before they had a chance to get a good look at me.

My watch showed I had just enough time to make it to the rendezvous before Ivo showed up, if I walked fast. Running would have attracted attention.

When I reached the spot, Katrina was standing huddled against a tree, looking very worried. She tried to smile when she saw me, and I saw her turn her eyes to the left. A tall, broad-shouldered goon was leaning against a tree, the tip of his cigarette growing brighter, then darker, very quickly. I came up close to Katrina and pretended to give her a kiss, at the same time pulling out Wilhelmina behind the tree. I think he knew what I was up to, because no sooner was Wilhelmina pointed when a piece of bark flew off the tree about a foot from my head. His second shot went wild and didn't appear to strike anything nearby. And then the big guy was flat on his back, a bullet where his cigarette had been. Katrina looked at me wide-eyed in protest, but she seemed to realize it was either him or us.

A few minutes later Ivo drove by, his headlights on low beam. He stopped at a traffic signal across from us, and I walked out into the street as if I were going to cross it. But I went right up to the orange Fiat behind him, knelt down pretending to look for something I had dropped, and slashed their front tire with Hugo. I hurried back to Katrina after the light had changed and both cars pulled away.

"Okay," I said, "let's go," and we walked over to the place we were to meet Ivo. He would have lost his tail by then—I hoped.

I pulled Katrina along. "There's Ivo," she said, pointing. There was no orange Fiat. He pulled over and parked. We unloaded the packs and left the boxes.

"I'm sorry I got you into this, Ivo," she said.

"Katrina, I am your friend," he replied.

"You *must* leave the country, Ivo," I said halfheartedly. It was probably a waste of words; he would never leave no matter what we said.

I started to walk across to the station, not without misgivings. The station might be full of OZNA or whoever had been chasing us. Katrina didn't move. I turned around. "Well, are you coming?" I asked. I watched Ivo drive off. No one followed.

"We're not taking the train," she said.

"What are we going to do then, walk?"

"No, Jesse James. Bring your pack." She began walking down the block, but stopped in front of a car about twenty feet from the corner. For a second I didn't move, then I shouldered my pack and followed her.

"Katrina," I said. "It won't do to keep holding out on me any longer. We could get into some very tricky situations."

"Always worrying, Mr. Jesse James, aren't you?" she said, opening the car door and climbing in after we had jammed our packs into the tiny car.

"Are we still going to the mountains," I asked, "or are we going fishing instead?"

"Oh, fishing," she said, fumbling with the key.

"Good," I said, "there's nothing I like more than sitting on a rock all day and catching fish."

"We are going to the mountains still, Jesse James. Why are you so untrusting?" She finally got the car started.

"Good," I said, ignoring her question, "I need some exercise."

She continued. "We are German-speaking Swiss tourists," she said.

"Sure."

"Good. You'll find your passport in the glove compartment."

I looked at it. It was a pretty good forgery but hardly up to AXE standards.

"We are Swiss tourists, newlyweds going on a backpacking trip in exotic Yugoslavia to get away from too many relatives."

"Sounds like fun," I said as we pulled out into traffic.

CHAPTER IX

It was a dark and rainy drive to Sremska Mitrovica. The rain began in earnest as soon as we got in the car. All I could see out of the rain-splattered window was lightning flashing high up in the black clouds and the momentarily blinding light from the headlights of oncoming cars. We didn't say much. Katrina concentrated on her driving and on her thoughts, and I looked out the windows dwelling on my own.

It was still dark and raining when we arrived at the railway station. We struggled to get the packs out of the car and ran across the parking lot to the station. It was damp and cool inside, and though the station wasn't large by any means, it had an empty, cavernous feeling because there were only a dozen people about. We took our places among the wooden benches.

We had been sitting about five minutes when a pretty woman in a white raincoat marched up to within about ten feet of us. She stopped and unleashed a German shepherd, which bounded over happily to Katrina. The woman didn't say anything; she turned and went and sat on a bench opposite us.

"This is Grusha, my dog. I haven't seen her in four days," Katrina whispered. I examined the dog, a healthy and good-looking female with what looked like good breeding. She was overjoyed to see Katrina. No barking, so I thought she must be well trained.

I looked around the station uneasily.

Abruptly Katrina said, "So tell me what you think? Can I bring her with us?" I looked at her surprised and then at the dog once more. "If you think it might spoil things I won't take her," Katrina said. I was even more surprised that she had asked for an unbiased opinion.

"How long are we going to be in the mountains?" I asked.

"Four or five days. We have plenty of food. She is well trained."

"I can see that," I said. I thought it over. It really wasn't a bad idea. We'd be out in the open forest and mountains a long time and Grusha would be added protection.

"Okay," I said, "take her."

"You're kidding." She sounded surprised.

"I told you my opinion. Why waste time?" She looked at me carefully and then took her purse and turned it around. The woman who brought the dog got up and left without saying a word. A man in a blue beret and dressed like a worker came up and sat a few yards away. He opened a schedule and looked it over impatiently. I watched as she hooked the car keys onto the dog's collar. She moved her eyes slightly, looking at the man, and the dog moved over to the man, who removed the keys while petting her. A minute later he looked at his watch, then got up and left.

"Why is it all right to take the dog?" asked Katrina.

"The breed is right, the age is right, and the training is right. And I'd like to know if we've got company as soon as possible," I said. She actually seemed to soften a bit toward me. The truth was, I already had plans for Grusha.

Five minutes later the train arrived. I was in for a surprise. We weren't going to ride in a passenger car. Instead, as it came into the station, we walked to the very end of the train.

"We are not Swiss," said Katrina, "but we are newlyweds. I'm going to call the man we meet 'uncle.' We are Serbs. Otherwise everything is the same."

I said, "Okay," but didn't like it. A lot of people would remember us.

At the last moment we were ushered aboard the caboose. It was an old car, darkly lit with ancient yellow lamps, and permeated by smells of smoke, wine, coffee, and the men who spent their hours there. There were no bunks, but leather couches had been pushed against all the walls of the two compartments into which the car was divided. Katrina's "uncle" introduced us. When they heard we were newlyweds, our reception was even heartier and all the more enthusiastic. We spent the next hours being toasted and bearing the brunt of newlywed jokes.

After I had five or six glasses of wine I decided to show Katrina a bit of affection. She was becoming loud and boisterous, and finally relaxing a little after so many days of tension. One of the old graybeards even serenaded us accompanying himself on the gusle, the ancient Slav single-strained violin.

Katrina used the opportunity to slip free of my friendly clutches and dance with every man aboard. Pretty soon she was sitting across from me patting some guy on the knee. I decided to get some air and went out and stood between the cars. I took a deep breath and filled my lungs with the cool damp air.

"A beautiful woman, your wife." I turned to see I had been joined by three of the trainmen, who had come out to smoke.

"Yes," I said, "she is lovely."

"It is good to begin a marriage in the country," said the graybeard. "The soul has room to breathe, to quiet itself, and commune with nature."

"Yes," I said.

"I am happy that you agree," the old man replied.

"You want to get off at Visoko?" asked a younger trainman, changing the subject. I nodded.

"We don't normally stop there. You will have to be ready and get off quickly. It's against regulations to stop."

"We appreciate your help. Katrina really wants to see her relatives there."

"I thought she said old school friend?"

"Yes, well she is a little embarrassed that she misses her family so much."

"Oh, sure, I understand. After all she is married now and will not see them often."

We rejoined the rest of the crew. There was more singing and dancing. Toward morning everyone dozed, exhausted from the night's revelry. I awoke earlier than the rest and went out to see what morning was like. Grusha came with me and soon had her muzzle stuck out in the wind. The sky had cleared during the night and the whole landscape had that fresh appearance you see only after a rain. I watched the lime-green fields roll by. It was nice to see a bit of the country.

"You son-of-a-bitch." I turned to see Katrina. "What did you tell those men about me? They looked at me very strangely."

"Nothing, Katrina. What could I tell them?" She looked at me skeptically.

"I'd like to know our destination. I've been put on the spot several times already. One of these days it's not liable to be that funny."

"We are getting off at Visoko," she said. Then she turned abruptly and went inside. I let out a deep breath.

Three hours later we arrived. Katrina and I stood at the end of the car with our packs on, waiting for the train to pull up. Katrina told me they were actually letting us off a little past Visoko so there wouldn't be any trouble with the station master. A quarter mile past the tiny village the train braked to a stop. The train already was moving again by the time we clambered down the embankment.

"It's a twelve-mile walk to Sarajevo. We couldn't very well have taken the train into the station. It might be watched. We'll rent a car there."

The rest of the walk was uneventful. We reached the outskirts of Sarajevo and then walked into the central city. The city was a center of Turkish authority when the Turks occupied much of Yugoslavia, until the last century, and it had a pronounced oriental flavor. I noticed several mosques as well as Christian churches. Katrina seemed to know where she wanted to go and it soon became apparent that we were going to a car rental office. I agreed to go and rent the car myself while Katrina waited at an outdoor café. I decided to use my Belgian passport rather than the Swiss papers Katrina had given me. Everything went smoothly until it came time to actually pick up the car. I was told I'd have to wait a half an hour until the car was serviced. I walked out the door into the bright sunlight, when I saw Jimmy Walker, one of the Company's residents in Yugoslavia. More importantly he saw me. I jaywalked across the street to meet him. There was nothing else I could do. We were, if not old friends, then long-time acquaintances. We shook hands, eyeing each other's big smiles. I had a problem, and I wondered if he had one. I tried to read it from his eyes, but he was a professional and I learned nothing.

"Nick, I'm amazed to find you in dull old Sarajevo. I won't ask what brings you our way. Hush, hush, I'm sure."

"You know why I'm here, Jimmy, as well as I do." I watched him flush. I knew then he had been told to keep an eye out for me. Probably every Company agent in Yugoslavia had been told that. I wondered how much he knew. He was probably just making the rounds. He'd have people in his pay at the pinch points of the city—the railway station, bus depot, and airport. What worried me was that some of them also might work for OZNA.

Suddenly it occurred to me how to test him. I'd walk him right by Katrina. If he recognized her, then I'd have to find a way to get out of this. Katrina was waiting a block away. We started walking along together.

"You know, Jimmy, AXE and the Company

don't always see eye to eye, but we are on the same side, aren't we, old buddy? And we both follow the Man's orders. I mean, interservice rivalry has gotten out of hand in the past."

"Nick, Nick, what a way to talk. Not only do we work for the same side, but you and I are old friends. We've never had any problems with you, Nick; it's David Hawk. The guy has a strange attitude. He may have said some things to the Man that weren't in his sister service's interest, but that's done and forgotten."

"I'm glad to hear that, Jimmy, because, for example, if you were to inadvertently blow my mission, I'd come here and have a talk with you."

"Nick, Nick, how could you even suggest such a thing? This is your old friend, Jimmy, not some thug you don't know. We're on the same side, buddy. Hey, remember those dancers in Morocco? What a night! You and me struggling against international Communism, side by side, shoulder to shoulder, for a better world."

We walked by Katrina. He looked her over, pausing at all the right places, but otherwise showed no sign of recognizing her. I supposed he had not been told much more than to keep a lookout for me. Katrina betrayed no emotion, but I could tell by her rigid posture that she was worried. I gestured for her to stay put as subtly as I could.

"Nick, let's stop in a bar and have a couple of drinks." I had been wondering how to deal with Jimmy and his invitation looked like the way out of my problem.

"Yeah, let's have a drink," I said. I planned to make sure I picked the bar. We walked a couple of blocks and saw a likely place.

The bar was old, dark, and large. The floor was white tile. I couldn't tell what color the walls had once been. When we arrived it was open but empty. We sat ourselves down at a large round table with ironback chairs and ordered a bottle of hundred-proof Sljivovica, Yugoslavian plum brandy. We drank it straight.

"Nick, this interservice rivalry thing is very bad. The Company would do anything to help you. Why don't you tell your old friends what we can do? Why let one unreasonable man—oh, David Hawk is a great man, I admit—but why let one man stand between you and the friendship we feel for you? Europe, Africa, South America—we've helped people everywhere."

"Yeah, a couple of them even survived the experience."

"Nick, that's no way to talk. I can promise you carte blanche. Just let us know what's going on."

"Jimmy, I had some trouble at the airport."

"I don't know anything about that, Nick."

"Just relay a little message for me. Anything strange happens on this mission and we'll have to assume there's a leak—a hole—in the Company, because in our heart of hearts we know you wouldn't do this deliberately. Jimmy, I will personally see that Angus Kourpart gets the message."

"Damn it, Nick, that goes against the Understanding, you know that. Hawk agreed in the best interest of the whole intelligence community not to do or say anything that will set Angus off again. The whole eastern European division would be dismantled and sent to Patagonian Station to cool their heels until he returns."

"Listen, Jimmy, if anything happens to me a coded message goes from poor dead Nick Carter to Angus Kourpart."

"Nick, the man is crazy. Everyone knows that."

"Just keep your nose clean, Jimmy, because if something happens it's going to be an issue, and you know how Hawk likes issues."

"Nick, Hawk—he's nearly as crazy as Angus. He won't cooperate. Why?"

"Well," I said, "for one thing, none of you guys can hold your liquor." He flushed beet red, of course. We had already finished half the bottle. Drinking it straight, a shot at a time, Russian style, does things to the brain. From then on he was determined to drink me under the table. Not an easy task. I figured two bottles and he'd be out for the twelve or fifteen hours I wanted him out. Unfortunately for me, Jimmy was quite a drinker. We had finished the second bottle and he was still solid. I told him about my latest adventures in Nairobi, about the lady with waterfall legs, about the Tin Pot dictator and his pet alligators, about taking a bullet from a colleague. He told me the usual lies about his sexual conquests, about the ladies who chased him down the street asking for more. We had a fine time.

He was still trying to convince me to cooperate when he got a strange expression on his face. He stopped midsentence. I decided it was time for a few quick toasts to hurry things along. Three quick ones, and his irises rolled up to the ceiling and stayed there. He swayed around in a small circle as if his muscles had gone out of gear and his backbone was the only thing keeping him upright. Then, he jerked slightly and flopped to the floor.

There was barely an inch left in the third bottle.

I wasn't feeling so good myself. I started to stand and found myself on an earth-size merry-go-round. I decided to make a strategic retreat and sat back down—heavily. When I saw the table at eye level, I suddenly realized why I had landed so hard; at least I was sitting on the floor. Jimmy was lying on it. But I was still convinced that I was more sober than I appeared. I thought for a minute. My feet felt numb, like they had gone to sleep. I was very tired and I wasn't sure I could make it to the door.

Suddenly Katrina was there. I told her to pay the bartender to put Jimmy in the back room. I also gave her a few more orders, but she was speaking some kind of strange language I couldn't understand, and I understand a lot of languages.

I don't remember much about the next twelve hours. I do remember riding in a car and stopping over and over again by the side of the road. I don't remember exactly what for. I remember seeing a bit of landscape, mountains, great forests, rugged, rocky-looking areas. I realized later that we were in the rugged mountain country on the border between Bosnia and Montenegro. The Fox and his partisans had once fought the Nazis here.

I vaguely remembered the car leaving. I know because I no longer felt the hum of the engine and everything became cold, quiet, and completely dark. I awoke the next morning with a terrible headache, stuffed none too completely into a sleeping bag. I knew the whole world hated me, but I forced myself up to look around. No Katrina. I thought she had just dumped me, but then I found both packs leaning neatly against a tree. Since I was up, I forced myself to do a little more looking around. I found that although I seemed to be in a deep forest, a small back road was only a hundred yards away. I walked carefully back to the packs and got myself some aspirin and gulped them down with water from the canteen. Then I got out the little gas stove and painfully assembled it, to make myself some coffee. Within an hour I was leaning back against a tree feeling better. Katrina arrived just before noon on foot, looking the way I wanted to feel.

CHAPTER X

"Well, Jesse James, I see you have managed to wake up. I'm really glad that you were sent to protect a naive young idealist like myself. Did we have a little too much to drink with our little friend yesterday?"

"It was not social drinking. And withering sarcasm doesn't become you," I said evenly.

"It didn't look very social when I got there. One of you was lying on the floor, the other was sitting on it. Maybe it would have gotten social if I'd arrived a couple of minutes later. Then both of you would have been lying on the floor together. Maybe your friend misses you even now."

"He is not a friend. He works for a Western intelligence agency."

"He seemed very intelligent. His expression as he lay on the floor was most thoughtful."

"You complain when I was forced to kill two men, and then you complain again when I go through a terrible ordeal in order to use nonviolent means. The son-of-a-bitch could hold his liquor better than I figured, that's all."

"Why don't you get yourself ready to move. You *can* move, can't you, Jesse James?"

"Of course I can move. I'm fine." Grusha came over and nuzzled my face. Katrina looked me over thoughtfully.

"Maybe I'd better fix you some breakfast, something light. You must be weak. I have never seen a man throw up so many times."

"I'm fine, really," I said. "But I don't have much of an appetite at the moment."

"That man was a Western agent? Then why was he a danger to us?"

"He's from a friendly but rival agency. I just wanted to make sure no problems developed. Your father did ask for only one man. And you never know how secure the other guy's operation is."

"You mean, he is like—British?"

"Something like that." I couldn't very well tell her he was American.

"I'm going to fix you some breakfast," she said. She started rummaging through the packs. "Some soft-boiled eggs, perhaps. I still don't understand why you were afraid of him."

"Suppose there are leaks. Suppose his organization had been penetrated and he makes a routine report about meeting me. There might be other reasons as well. It's a kind of complicated profession."

"Then CRML might learn where we are, when before they knew nothing."

"I was trying to give us twenty-four hours."

"Then we should get moving soon."

"Right," I said. I decided to rest my eyes.

The next thing I knew she was shaking me awake, holding a plate in front of me. I reached for it and she brought me over a cup of coffee. I was suddenly very hungry.

It did not take us long to get our gear together. I slung my pack on my back and felt the sixty-five pounds press down uncomfortably on my back and shoulders, but then I tightened the belt and it shifted to my waist. I looked at the hardwood forest around me. It was not only good cover but beautiful to look at. We headed south, up a gradual slope keeping to the forest.

Our pace was somewhat ragged at first, but soon we were into a smooth, even rhythm. I actually began feeling good. We followed a stream up the hillside, stepping from boulder to boulder. I watched the green and white water gurgling beneath us. I stopped at one point, and knelt down and cupped my hand into the icy water again and again, drinking deeply. I was still badly dehydrated from all the booze. The water tasted clean and sweet, magical and unprocessed. I splashed some on my face, took a deep breath and pushed myself to my feet. We had to keep moving.

The next hours were uneventful. We continued to climb the gradual slope mostly through deep forest. I could begin to see the edges now; the forest thinned as we climbed higher. All around we were ringed with rugged mountains, barren, rocky, with sparse lime-green meadows. We hadn't even reached the high country. The landscape was growing wilder, harsher, and more barren. Finally, late in the afternoon, we stopped for our long-postponed lunch. Katrina picked a quiet place deep in the forest among the tallest trees, far from the stream. Grusha padded around us, happily sniffing roots.

Katrina broke out a lunch of cheese, bread and sausages.

"One thing I am afraid of," she said. "There are

wolves in these mountains, many of them."

"Wolves are fine creatures," I said. "I'd sooner kill a man than a wolf."

"They are evil. They carry off children and sheep and eat the bodies of the dead. There were not many until the last war."

"All myths," I said. "Wolves are more honest than men, more loyal, and work together more peacefully than we do."

"These wolves have acquired a taste for human flesh. At one time there were many corpses scattered in these mountains. Thousands upon thousands left unburied. The Nazis had no respect for the fallen, and the partisans had no time. The population of wolves exploded. Many have since been killed, so now they go hungry because we have peace."

"Wolves and men would live peacefully together except that sheep come between them," I said. "Sheep make it a war. It is the same way with secret agencies. If the sheep did not come between us, we would live in peace with each other, in mutual respect and love. Besides, it's better to be eaten by wolves than maggots or slow worms."

"That is a lot of nonsense. You are a little bit crazy in the head, Jesse James. You like wolves because you yourself are like them."

"I take that as a compliment," I said, "but there is nothing to be afraid of. Grusha has sharp eyes and ears. She'll warn us if a pack comes near." The dog, hearing her name, came over and stuck her nose at me. I gave her a testy pat on the head. Then it was time to get moving again.

We stood up, brushed ourselves off, and hoisted on our packs.

"You go first," she said. "I might get frightened

and kill some innocent wolf."

Again, I fell into the familiar rhythm of movement. We skirted the mountaintop and began walking downhill, but deeper into wild country. We stopped at an outcropping. I searched the 160° arc visible from there with my binoculars. I saw a buck break into a run on a high, distant meadow. I saw some small animals scurry about, but there were no signs of the two-legged kind.

It was getting late and, although spring days are long, already becoming cooler. We headed down into the shallow valley and started up a still larger mountain. Grusha ran up the trail ahead of us.

"It's best to keep her back here with us. Someone might see her before we see them," I said.

"Oh, let her run. We have kept her with us all day. Even a German shepherd gets restless."

"Okay, but just for a few minutes." I frankly didn't think it would do that much harm. "You promised not to be sentimental about the dog."

"I keep my promises, Jesse James."

"The forest gives an illusion of safety. If they have the men and technology, and want us badly enough, they can find us," I said.

She said nothing.

I heard Grusha barking loudly. I can recognize barks. Some are happy, some frightened. This was the serious kind. I jogged up the trail as quickly as I could. The trail ran beside a steep chasm that was becoming deeper with every step I took. I ran another one hundred yards along the edge of the steep stream, when I rounded the bend and saw the barking Grusha facing a large brown bear. The dog was already covered with blood. Its tail was slung below. Its teeth were bared, its back sloped. I unholstered Wilhelmina. Katrina ran up beside me. I saw her reach for her pistol. I knocked the gun wide, just in time. The shot went wide.

"You can't kill a bear with that, you'll just anger it." I unhooked my pack, dropped it, and moved forward. I fired twice in the air. I moved in for a kill shot, but I knew that a pistol, even Wilhelmina, was no weapon against an enraged bear. With one swipe the bear knocked Grusha over the edge of the cliff. I fired in the air again, and the bear, satisfied with its handiwork, bounded off, fear of man still being stronger than its anger. Then I saw the cub, lurking in a thicket. It moved off in pursuit of its mother.

Katrina was leaning over the cliff's edge screaming. "Grusha, Grusha!" I peeked over to see how Grusha was doing. I expected to see her lying among the rocks and whitewater rushing forty feet below us. Instead she was on a narrow ledge, whimpering and trying to get her footing. But her back feet hung over the edge. I intended to go and get the climbing rope, but I saw her start to slip off. I examined the cliff face as carefully as I could, looking for something to grab hold of. I saw a crevice and a small bush a few feet above the ledge. Not good, but it would have to do. I flipped myself over the cliff using both hands the way a tumbler would. Katrina must have been surprised as hell. But I wanted to be sure of facing the cliff and falling close to it feet first. I figured I might survive the fall if I missed the ledge or slipped off it.

It was kind of like sky diving. I hit the ledge hard. I felt my knee give and pushed myself hard against the cliff face, fighting desperately for balance. I yanked the little shrub right out of the cliff.

I was going over, already imagining the black rocks and whitewater welcoming committee. But my fist jam in the crevice held. I pulled the foot that was sticking out in the air back on the ledge.

I looked over at Grusha. I replaced my left hand with my right and reached down with the freed left and grabbed her by the collar, pulling her back completely on the ledge.

"Get the rope," I yelled to Katrina. I saw her disappear out of view.

"Stay, Grusha, stay!" I said to the whimpering dog. If she moved, all my good work would be for nothing. "Be brave!" I exhorted her. It was a silly thing to say, but she was frightened and hurt and I thought the authoritative voice might help calm her. Katrina still had not brought the rope. The terrified dog tried to inch toward me, but the cliff was too narrow and she slipped. I reached down again and grabbed her by the collar.

"Stay, Grusha, stay!"

"Nick, here is the rope." I watched the green and purple climbing rope snake down the cliff.

"More," I shouted. "Wrap your end around a tree but don't tie it."

Now came the fun part—leaning down and tying the rope around Grusha in the form of a sling. I would have been happier if my piece of the ledge had been a little wider. I didn't like feeling my heels hanging out in midair. I slid my hand lower in the crevice. It narrowed so much that I switched to a hand jam. It would have been easier, but my piece of ledge and Grusha's were separated by a foot-long chunk of thin air. I talked to the dog, patted her on the head a few times, and went to work. I had to stretch a long way to reach around the dog's middle. I had slipped the rope most of the way around her when my hand brushed over one of her cuts. The dog whined and moved back, looking at me like I was a traitor. I started over.

I got the rope around the dog on the second try, but now I had to wrap it around again. First I straightened up and rested a minute. The second wrapping was no easier than the first, but soon I had it done and turned my attention to completing the sling.

When my work was finished, I looked up for Katrina. She wasn't there.

"Katrina, where are you?"

"Back by the trees," came the answer.

"No. Come forward to the edge of the cliff so you can see. Take one end of the rope in your left hand and the other in your right. Pull the dog up with one hand and then tighten the slack in the rope with the other." She got the idea quickly. I grabbed the dog and helped to hoist her up as far as I could. Katrina hauled away. Grusha made a whimpering ascent. I waited. Some time later, green and purple rope slid down next to my face.

"Just tie it securely to a tree," I yelled.

"Okay."

I leaned out and more or less walked straight up the cliff. When I pulled myself over, I suddenly felt warm arms around me.

"You saved Grusha!" There were tears in her eyes. "How can you be so brave to jump over a cliff to save a dog?" I gave her a big smile and reached my hand around her beautiful rear, but she seemed not to notice. I let her go and went over to take a look at Grusha. I felt along her legs and ribs. She whimpered a lot, but I couldn't find anything broken.

"Is she all right?"

"I think so." I looked up at the sky. The clouds were already pink.

"I must clean her and dress her wounds."

"No. We must find a spot to camp. You can take care of her there. We have to climb to the next shelf of the mountain where it's flat. We can reach water and camp there." I gestured to the cliff.

She cooed over Grusha awhile. Then we got our packs and started up the rough trail. But Grusha just lay there and wouldn't move. I walked back, squatted down, and pulled her into my arms. Then I started up the steep trail, holding the dog in front. All the way up the trail, Grusha licked my face.

CHAPTER XI

We struggled up the steep trail. Grusha was feeling heavier and heavier with each step. Part of the problem was the sixty-five-pound pack I was carrying on my back. Although Katrina hadn't said anything, she had been giving me different looks than she had before.

"That bear, why didn't you shoot it?"

"Not a good option."

"You kill men without compunction."

"The bear was only trying to protect her cub. Besides, a 9mm is no weapon to shoot a bear with. It might have stopped the bear in its tracks, and you and I were standing next to the edge of the cliff."

"You could've shot that killer bear right between the eyes."

"You've been watching too many westerns," I said. I started to explain but decided to let it drop. "You're beginning to sound like a gun moll. Shoot this, kill that. And Grusha here is getting heavy."

"Well, set her down. I don't know how you can carry her. We can make camp here."

"It's not a good place. Where could we get water?"

Katrina looked over at the stream from which the path was now diverging. It was obviously too steep to reach. She was a smart lady, she didn't argue the point. I labored up a rocky, nearly vertical section of trail. I forced my legs to take step after heavy step.

When we reached the first level ground I set the dog down. Katrina took off her pack and began cooing over the beast. I started looking around for a place to camp.

"Come on, Katrina, we must find a campsite before it gets dark."

"What's wrong with here? It is a beautiful clearing and there is more light here."

"Exactly. We're going over to the dense part of the forest." I pointed where the woods looked the darkest and started off. She reluctantly put on her pack and followed.

"It's so dark."

"That's why we must hurry." It did not take long to find a comfortable-looking spot on the pine-needle-covered ground. I hurried Katrina off to the stream a hundred yards away to do some dog repair work.

I strung up the tarp that we were using for cover and unpacked the sleeping bags. I dug a small pit in the dark for a campfire and then lined it carefully with stones from a dry stream bed. I hung a small tarp high above the fire to scatter the small amount of smoke even before it reached the thick tree branches above us.

In a few minutes Katrina returned with Grusha in tow. "Grusha does not seem so bad, Nick. You were so brave. I'll never forget how you just leaped over the cliff. I appreciate what you did."

"I'm fond of animals," I said. She had finally begun to call me Nick. "Now how about dinner?"

While she started to fix supper I decided to take a look around. I grabbed my binoculars and hurried off. I walked down to the stream and washed off. Grusha had managed to bleed all over me, and I had a few scrapes of my own. I took several deep drinks of the icy water. Then I started looking around. I hoped to find a lookout to survey the terrain from. The idea was to see trouble before it saw us. I stumbled through some brush, frightening a doe. She sprinted off with a flourish of white tail deeper into the woods.

Ten minutes later I was about to give up, when I noticed a tall tree in the center of a clearing. It was better than nothing—how much better, I wouldn't know until I reached the top. I climbed up through the sticky branches as high as I could. The sky was deep blue in twilight, but the forest below me looked dark and ominous. I took out my binoculars and surveyed what I could, which wasn't a great deal. I did notice a nearby rocky outcropping that I decided to climb the first thing in the morning.

It was getting too dark to see anything more, so I climbed down and made my way back to camp.

"Where were you? You almost missed dinner." Katrina served a hearty dinner of skewered lamb and vegetables, the last of the fresh meat. About halfway through the meal I took off my shirt. It hadn't dried yet and I felt uncomfortable in its dampness. I moved closer to the fire.

"You will get cold."

I explained that it was an old American Indian trick, that the radiant heat from the fire would keep you warmer without clothes. I invited her to try it.

"You look like a half-naked Indian," she said. "You even look a little red in the firelight."

"Try it, you'll like it," I encouraged her.

"Maybe after dinner I will surprise you," she said, with a smile. "If I do it now my food will get cold."

The truth was, it was getting a bit nippy out. While radiant heat will do the trick, it takes a big fire. The Indians used about half a tree. My back was freezing. Pretty soon the goose bumps would appear. I continued my coaxing.

"You certainly are a beautiful woman."

"You still want me to take off my shirt, poor Jesse James," she said, finishing up her meal. "If it works so well, why do you still have your pants on?" she asked. I quickly slipped off my pants and resumed eating my dinner.

"I'm not a schoolgirl," she said as she slipped off her blouse. She stood there a second as if waiting for something to happen.

"Would it work better if I took off more?"

"Oh, yes," I said, "much better." She unhooked her bra, letting her magnificent breasts hang free. Her nipples crinkled up in the night air.

"Should I take off my pants too? Would that work better, too?"

"Oh, yes," I said, "much better." She undid her belt and unzipped her jeans.

"You're sure?" she asked.

"Absolutely."

"You know what, Mr. Jesse James?"

"No, what?" I said innocently.

"I think that if I take off my pants, my backside

is going to be as cold as yours." She laughed happily, grabbed up her stuff, and went over to her sleeping bag.

"Come, Grusha," she said. "Oh, yes, do the dishes. I cooked the dinner." She laughed and laughed as she slipped off her pants and climbed into her sleeping bag. Any man with less self-control than I have would have thrown something. I just sat there. This one was a tease. Finally, I walked over to her sleeping bag. I reached over and touched her on the shoulder. She turned around slowly and I found myself looking down the barrel of her small, pearl-handled pistol.

"That doesn't look like a socialist pistol to me."

"It's a revisionist pistol. If you don't stop, your body may end up in this sleeping bag but your brains are going to end up over by the fire." At that moment Grusha growled at me. For now she was not my friend.

"You're very pretty, Mr. Jesse James," she said, looking me over, "but you take me for granted."

"You wouldn't shoot me," I said. "It would ruin your mission." I reached over and gently slipped the gun from her hand, keeping my eyes on her eyes. I reached down and unzipped the sleeping bag.

"I'll shoot you after the mission," she said firmly.

"Yes, maybe," I said, unzipping the bag further.

"Don't."

I zipped the bag back up. "Fortunately for you, I'm not the bad guy you take me for. I went over and poured water in the dirty dishes and put out the fire. When I walked over to her, she turned her back to me and said nothing. I decided to play her game. I slipped into my sleeping bag and lay on my back a long time listening to the sounds of the night until I fell into a deep sleep.

I was on my way to the outlook before dawn. I had dressed quietly and put on my tennis shoes but took nothing with me except my binoculars and Wilhelmina. Grusha followed. I tried to drive her back to camp, but it was no use so I let her come along. I moved through the dark woods at a quick light, stepping jog. I could barely hear my feet touch the pine needles.

It didn't take me long to reach the base of the cliff I had seen the night before. I thought Grusha would never make it up, but there was an easy passage through the rocks I hadn't noticed.

It was not yet sunrise when I reached the outcropping. Soon dawn extended her rosy fingertips around the distant mountains. When it became light enough I put the binoculars to my eyes and began a systematic survey of the countryside. I saw a fox skirt a clearing in the valley below. Minutes later, a chamois—a small, goatlike antelope prized by hunters—moved slowly, grazing peacefully on the distant mountain slope. I saw what looked like the back end of a boar disappear into a thicket, but I saw no sign of any two-legged beings. I stretched out on the rock. Grusha lay down beside me. I watched for a long time without moving, hoping to catch sight of the breakfast campfire.

Soon my stomach told me it was time to return to camp.

"Jesse James likes to wander," Katrina said when I walked up. I wondered what had happened to being called Nick.

* * *

We had been on the trail for about an hour when we reached a small stream that we followed up the mountainside. We jumped from stone to stone above the crystal clear, icy-cold water. Grusha padded along in the water and stopped periodically, shaking herself all over us. It was a hard climb, but from the security standpoint, safer than following an established path. After thirty minutes of climbing we emerged high on the mountainside. Katrina pointed to a distant mountain another range over.

"You see that spot? My father and the Fox retreated through those mountains during the war. There are eight thousand buried over there. Thousands more left unburied. Is it any wonder we have wolves?"

We walked across the clearing. I stopped at the edge and surveyed. But it wasn't until I examined a distant hillside that I saw the first sign of another human being. I told Katrina where to look and handed her the glasses.

"Shepherd, probably," she said. "There are still some in these mountains. Once many more people lived up here, some to escape the Turks and eventually to escape various other occupiers, but as things got better below they abandoned the harsh life of the mountains for the more fertile lowlands."

I hadn't seen any signs of a flock. But that in itself proved nothing. I hoped Katrina was right. "Let's go," I said pensively.

"You worry too much, Mr. Jesse James. I thought you were concentrating on other things." She gave me a smile.

"Don't remind me," I said. "Come, let's go."

The bright day had begun to turn a little cloudy. We skirted the summit of the mountain and circled down a steep slope to the col between the next mountains. Soon we were picking our way up still another slope.

"You don't pick an easy route," I said.

"Can you imagine a whole army moving through terrain like this, hungry, attacked on all sides, carrying thousands of wounded with them? Do you think we will give up the country this time without a fight?"

"I'm a big supporter of patriotism myself."

"Ah, you don't understand—if our country were the same size as yours, imagine the equivalent number of people that would have been killed."

We walked a while in silence. I broke it first.

"When will we reach our destination?" I asked.

"Tomorrow."

"When's lunch?" I was getting hungry with all this exercise.

"A couple of hours." The terrain was easier the next mile or so; we were back in the world of woods and streams again. I saw a marten near a small cascade. Then we began to climb steeply straight up the side of the mountain. Katrina had to stop more and more frequently to catch her breath. The forest began to thin. The trees grew shorter and shorter until they were no higher than bushes. Finally they stopped altogether and we emerged into the world of rocks.

"We'll stop around the other side for lunch," Katrina said. I nodded. We climbed through a field of large boulders until we reached a steep cliff. "Up there," said Katrina. It looked bad but like a lot of climbs was not actually as hard as it appeared. I only had to use my hands once or twice, although I did have to boost Grusha up in a couple of places. From the edge it looked like another rocky meadow filled with the same large boulders we had seen before, but suddenly I stopped and took a closer look. The rocks had been carved into what looked like large sarcophaguses. They were man-size in length and about the same height. Some had peaked roofs like little houses. They were all decorated with carved bas-reliefs—hunting scenes, people walking and dancing, battles, weddings, and celebrations. The figures were elongated and skinny like those you see in gothic cathedrals.

"What the hell are these things?" I asked Katrina.

"Bogomil graves," she replied. "There are many all over Bosnia."

"But what are they doing here? This is one of the remotest places in the country."

"You know who the Bogomils were?"

"Vaguely."

"They were a mysterious Christian sect during the middle ages, but because they were heretics, they were persecuted by everyone, both Christians and Moslems. They were mostly poor people, peasants, shepherds, and small landowners. They were driven deeper and deeper into these mountains by the awful persecutions. Eventually they died out. No one is sure what they believed, but some say they thought there were two gods, one good and the other evil, who struggled eternally for dominance. That's the way they explained how evil the world is. The bad god was winning."

"Yeah," I said. "It's all coming back to me. I was just surprised to see the tombs here. I remember reading that they disappeared five or six centuries ago."

"Yes. They reemerged in different parts of the world called by different names—in Egypt, in Asia Minor, and in the south of France. They were a very ancient sect. Some say the holy ones or priests abstained from meat and sex. And when they became ill they took a mysterious sacrament and then fasted until death took them."

"Very nice," I said. "Probably why they died off."

"Take a look around. I've seen the tombs before. I'll fix lunch."

I wandered around looking at the tombs. Most were like the ones I had first seen, as tall as a man with peaked roofs, but others were table high and flat like the one Katrina was seated on to make lunch. Most of the flat-topped tombs had carvings of men with beards looking very intent and serious.

We were in a hidden hollow high above the valley floor and surrounded on three sides by either peaks or low cliffs. The only way to spot us was from the air. I sat down, leaned back against a tomb, and stretched my legs and relaxed in the warm sun. I was glad it hadn't clouded over completely yet. Grusha was lying next to me gnawing on an uninteresting piece of wood. I felt good. For a moment I wanted to believe there was no mission, just Grusha and this beautiful woman.

But it was time to move on.

CHAPTER XII

We edged down the mountain. What goes up must come down, they say. It is certainly true of trekking through mountains. When we stopped to rest a few minutes later, I noticed that Grusha's cuts had become infected. I didn't say anything to Katrina. I figured we would take care of them when we stopped for the night.

"I think when we get up the next mountain we'll be able to walk along the ridgeline. It will be much easier."

"Good," I said.

"It's going to be a long day."

"No problem," I said. It didn't take us more than an hour to climb the next mountain. When we reached the narrow trail that ran along the ridgeline I stopped and put down my pack. I squatted down and looked at the tracks. Lug-sole boots, several pairs. These were not made by the shepherds that occupy these mountains.

"What's the matter?"

"A lot of traffic on this path. Maybe it's nothing, but keep your eyes open." I took out my binoculars and searched both directions. I didn't see anything, but I felt uneasy. The tracks were re-

115

cent. I studied the trail again. The ridgeline ran along a range of mountains that were lower than the others we had been on. There were small, scrubby trees along either side of the trail providing a little cover if you got off the trail. Looking to the right, I could follow the trail with my glasses at least a quarter of a mile, because the point we were on was a little higher than the intervening terrain. I studied the ridgeline further away. Several sections of trail were visible that were quite distant from where we stood.

"How long will we be on this trail?" I asked.

"At least four miles. Why? I don't see anyone, and we can make good time for a change. My legs are so tired from going up and down and up and down, again and again."

I walked along the trail and knelt several times to look at the tracks. The ground was rocky, so I had to go quite a distance.

"This trail is heavily used," I said to Katrina, as I walked back. "I think you should go on. I'll catch up with you. I'm going to have a look over that hill." I pointed to the mountain to our left. "I want to make sure no one is going to come along behind us. Keep your eyes open." She looked at me doubtfully, but she didn't argue. I watched her and Grusha head off, then hid my pack behind the stunted fir trees.

I jogged along the rough trail as quickly as I could until I reached the point where the trail ascended the peak. Then I slowed to a quick walk as I climbed the mountain. I crossed the summit quickly and started down the other side. I didn't like what I saw. Two men with hunting rifles were moving along the trail a hundred yards below me in the dip between the mountains. I ducked behind some rocks and looked into my binoculars. They seemed to be in no hurry. They had apparently come up a feeder trail that climbed to the ridge from the east. There was a trail closer to me angling down to the west where they might turn off. I noticed they weren't carrying packs, so I knew they must have camped somewhere to either side of the range. I watched for any signs that they were other than the innocent hunters they appeared to be—any special alertness or fear. But I couldn't tell from this distance.

I hoped they would take the west trail and solve my problems. Contrary to what Katrina had said, I don't like killing innocent civilians unless I have to. It can't always be helped. In espionage like in war, a lot of nice guys finish last. They had hunting rifles and I had a pistol, which didn't give me much room for chitchat. Given the nature of the trail I didn't see how I could allow them to follow along behind us unless I was sure they were hunters; otherwise we'd be sitting ducks. I was still moving down toward them, undecided whether to confront them in a friendly way and see what kind of reaction I got, or make a run for it. But then I saw something that stopped me in my tracks—two more hunters. The first two stopped at the west trail crossing, sat down heavily and broke out cigarettes. A minute later the other two joined them. It was time for me to move on. I had made my decision.

I climbed the hill quickly. When I reached the top I picked my way through the rocks, then went down as fast as I could. When I reached level ground I broke into a run to where I had left the pack.

I slung the pack on my back and started off

before I had even tied the belt. I began by walking quickly, but soon I broke into a slow, steady jog. I looked at my watch and tried to estimate how long I had to get out of sight before they reached the crest of the hill. I could see the point far ahead of me where the trail finally dipped behind some rocks. I knew how far I had to go.

It took me a while to realize I wasn't going to make it at the rate I was going. I went into the closest thing to a sprint you can do with a sixty-five-pound pack on your back. The trail was rocky. It took all of my concentration to watch my footing and keep my speed up. My feet and legs felt good the first couple of hundred yards but as I kept the pace going my legs began to feel like lead. I had to run faster. I gave it everything I had. It took so much effort my brain thought nothing but movement.

I slowed enough to look behind me. Nothing. I resumed my pace. A second later I was behind the rocks. I dropped to the ground panting heavily. After a couple of minutes I forced myself to crawl back and take a look. I didn't see anyone at first, but then a head followed by the rest of the body popped into view. They hadn't paused long. I turned and looked toward the direction I had to go, sizing up the situation. I slipped back down and grabbed my pack, and started off. It was nearly as far to the next outcropping as it had been to the last one. I decided that we had to get off the trail altogether and go cross country although it would be more difficult and would take more time.

I kept up the pace. My knees began to feel soft, like the insides were getting spongy, but I kept moving. I was panting when I reached the second outcropping. I had started to throw myself on the ground when I noticed what I least wanted to see. The trail doglegged; another stretch of it was visible from the first outcropping. I began to run again.

My chest felt like a burning accordion when I finally reached cover. I threw myself on the ground and did nothing but breathe for four or five minutes. Then I checked my watch. I estimated I would catch up with Katrina in about a half an hour; I pulled on my pack and started out once more.

I was so intent on catching Katrina that I nearly passed her. She and Grusha were hidden back in the stunted fir trees.

"In a hurry, Jesse James?" she called out softly. I saw her gun and reached for Wilhelmina.

"No, no, it's all right," she said. "I got the gun out when I heard you coming." I went over and sat down beside her.

"There are four men with hunting rifles moving along the trail behind us. We've got to find a safe place for tonight."

"I've seen people, too, a hunter, a couple backpacking. Maybe it means nothing, but how can I tell?" she said. She paused and then continued. "I think I know a place we can camp."

She took out a topographical map and pointed first to where we were and then to the campsite. I studied the contour lines. It was not going to be easy to reach, but judging from the map alone, the site she picked looked good, both secure and hidden.

"That way," I said, pointing west. I got up and got ready to move.

"But how do you know we can get down there?"

"With a rope I can get down any cliff in these mountains. Come on." We pushed our way through the thick, sticky trees for about fifty yards before we reached the edge of the cliff. I lay down on my stomach and leaned out as far as I could. It didn't look too bad. It was about fifty feet down and there was only one tricky outcropping to deal with.

"Can you rappel?" I asked.

"No. I know what it is, though."

"We don't have time for lessons. I'll lower you down. Don't worry about falling. Do worry about smashing into the rock face. Keep facing the cliff at all times and use your feet to push yourself away from it." I strapped the sling into place. "There is only one difficult spot. Take your time going over the outcropping. We may have to adjust the rope." I wrapped the rope around a small tree and got my footing. She just stood there, so I pointed to the edge of the cliff. She looked at me.

I gestured for her to get moving and she bravely climbed over the side. I leaned back and out over the cliff so I could keep an eye on her progress. Except for some complications in getting past the outcropping there were no problems.

Next it was Grusha's turn. I was impressed with the dog's steadiness. It could have been an absolute mess. As it was, the dog gave me only one bit of trouble, and that was up top when the rope rubbed on the bear's scratch. Grusha looked at me with big frightened eyes when I eased her over the cliff, but she didn't bark or whine. I had the same problem with the outcropping I had with Katrina, but she made it down okay. Then I lowered the packs.

I began to think things would be as smooth as silk when the packs caught. I had to clamber over the side myself. I tied off the rope but left some slack. I shinnied down the cliff and kicked the packs free of the cliff and started to climb back up when my feet slid out from under me. I slammed into the cliff but not too hard. There were no more problems. I rappeled down to join the rest of the expedition. I kicked myself out from the cliff face again and again as I let the rope slide me down.

We had gained a great deal of time by going over the cliff. The rest of the downhill was a scramble. The slope was steep and rocky, but the trees grew larger, giving us more room to maneuver. I slipped on some gravel and scraped my arm trying to get Grusha down some rocks.

"Poor Jesse James. But I have a nice surprise for you."

I gave her a friendly leer.

"You have only one thing on your mind. I meant the campsite."

"I'm sure it's a nice campsite," I said hoarsely.

"Oh, Jesse James, you are a little bit crazy," she said.

I don't know what I expected in the way of a campsite, but I smelled it before I saw it—the faint odor of rotten eggs. And then I saw the bubbling hot springs and three jade-green pools steaming in the cool air. Each pool flowed into the next lower one; then they joined a small freshwater stream. They were nestled together near the bottom of a cliff whose white rocks were covered with blue and green moss. Water lightly dripped from the moss-covered cliff into the stream. There was a small waterfall a few feet away that was probably as cold as the pools' water was hot.

"My father discovered this place. He was on patrol and they were cut off in a terrible storm. They were dressed lightly and would have frozen if they had not immersed themselves in the pools for nearly twenty-four hours until the storm had passed.

I took a closer look at the pools. I could see the water was bubbling up from springs at the bottom. They didn't actually smell that bad. In any case it was a small price to pay for a hot bath in the middle of nowhere.

"My father told no one about the place. He used to come here with my mother. He felt a little guilty, but he kept it as his secret. Look. It's so beautiful, and there is fresh water right nearby. You can rinse off in that little waterfall after you soak." She was as excited as a kid. Even Grusha barked happily.

I looked up at the sky, which was already a deep gray. "We'd better set up camp before we go splashing around."

It didn't take long, but we needed more wood, so I wandered off to gather some and have a look around. You have to know the lay of the land. The spot was beautiful, trees and grass and springs, and it was hidden, but it was also a potential trap. I wanted to make sure we had a back door. I searched along the base of the cliff until I found what I was looking for and then headed back to camp. Katrina's clothes were lying in a pile on the ground near her sleeping bag. I knew I was in for another nice surprise. I walked over to the pools and removed my own shoes and socks. I could see Katrina relaxing in the water.

"Hey, Jesse James," she said. She climbed out of the pool looking like a goddess. My body was like iron filings before a magnet. She walked over to me and stood over me smiling. I pulled her down beside me, sliding my hand down her glistening body. She leaned back on the grass, her back arched, her breasts heaving and sighing like the ocean's surf.

"I'm feeling so much like going to bed," she said. She gave a delicate yawn.

"You feel like going to bed," I said, "but I don't think you're sleepy." I slipped my hand down. Her spring was as hot and wet as the one a few yards away. I leaned over and gently kissed her mouth.

She reached over and ran her wet hand up and down the front of my pants, visibly pleased at what she found. I slipped out of my shirt and stood up to take off my pants. She helped by yanking at my pants cuff, and finally we discarded the briefs.

"What are these?" she asked, pointing to Pierre and Waldo.

"They are weapons, bombs," I said. "I can't exactly carry them around in my pocket."

She got up and ran over to the steaming pool. I went over to join her but brought Wilhelmina along.

"You like making love with bombs on, but what happens when you have a good time? Do they go off when you do?" She laughed. I reached over, grabbed her foot, and pulled her underwater and pushed her head down. She popped to the surface and was about to yell, but at the last minute she stopped herself. I figured even she knew enough was enough.

She looked at me appraisingly, then reached over and held my hand awkwardly for a second. "You're very pretty, Jesse James."

I reached over and grabbed her, taking her into my arms. She was slippery and wet. I pulled her underwater with me. I don't know how porpoises do it, but that was what it was like—all splashing water and all pleasure.

CHAPTER XIII

In the morning Katrina was all smiles. Last night's activities had finally brought our private little war to an end. She made us a hearty breakfast, tended Grusha's infection with care, and then helped me pack up.

The first part of the hike was steep, strewn with boulders, and overgrown with cranky vines that liked nothing better than to trip dogs and men. After trudging uphill for an hour and forty-five minutes we stopped at a level spot to rest.

Katrina pried off the cap on the end of her pack frame and pulled out a map. It was the first time she had shown me this particular one. It consisted of two parts, a map and an overlay. At first it was difficult to figure out how they were keyed to fit together. There must have been twenty or twenty-one lines on the transparent overlay. I knew most of them were meaningless, but I wasn't sure which.

After she showed me how to interpret the map, we spread it out on the ground and examined the route. It was a rough haul but not a long one, just under six miles. On the topographical map our destination looked like a classical, glaciated "hanging valley," which meant it ended high above the present valley floor. This one was shallow, the terrain wilder. We would have to climb the cliff at the end of the valley.

"My father has never been there, but the Fox told him there is an overgrown path." She pointed out a line with her fingernail, coming from a point on the ridge down into the valley. "That's the approach I had planned, but we were forced off the ridge trail. I'm not sure of the best way to get there now."

I examined the map carefully. "Okay," I said. "I've got it figured." I showed her the route. "We'll have to wait until we see part of it to be sure."

"Does it look like a likely location for a secret Nazi intelligence post?" she asked. I looked at the map again.

"Could be," I said.

We put on our packs and continued the climb.

"One question has been bothering me," I said. "How did the Nazis manage to get so many talented men to be traitors?"

"Do you know how complicated our country was during the war? When the Nazis invaded they found an unhappy, disorganized country; that's why it was easy for them at first. Some ethnic groups even welcomed the Nazis, thinking they could use them to destroy other groups they hated. The Fox headed one resistance group, but there were dozens—monarchists, Communists, nationalists—from each ethnic group. Sometimes these groups fought the Nazis, but just as often they fought each other. They betrayed each other to the Germans, even cooperated with the Nazis to form joint commands. There was terrible confusion.

"The Fox won not so much because he was a Communist but because only his group cut across all ethnic lines. He converted many people. Some had been collaborating with the Nazis, a few continued to do so. They were being blackmailed by the Nazis. The Nazis may have held their families, but whatever the reason, they betrayed the Fox. But they never confessed their crimes. Some were leading partisans slated for high office in the Fox's government. They lived many years in peace. Then somehow CRML got hold of a copy of the records detailing their collaboration with the Nazis and they blackmailed them. My father believes this happened in 1957, and he believes that CRML gave its records to the KGB.

"Here is the key: The Fox broke with Stalin in 1948 and purged all of Uncle Joe's supporters. Do you understand what that means?"

It was ringing big bells for me. I said: "The controlled ones escaped all the Fox's anti-Stalinist purges. They themselves didn't know in 1948 that they'd become traitors again."

"Exactly. This is why the Fox could trust no one but my father; he knew my father wasn't one."

"So suddenly the Fox discovered that all his tricks to eliminate CRML and the KGB had been for nothing. First he swallowed his pride and asked your father to help, then he swallowed his pride again and told your father to ask for our help."

"Yes," she said. "The controlled one who confessed to the Fox always felt guilty. My father believed he would have confessed sooner if the Fox had been more understanding; then they would have been exposed years ago. Anyway, this man knew there was a copy of the documents here, because he was at the intelligence post the night the Nazis pulled out. He even came back and checked to make sure they were here, but he didn't burn the documents; he reburied them. He planned to confess, all those years, but his courage failed him until he was on his deathbed."

"But didn't he know who the other controlled ones were?" I asked.

"He wouldn't say. We have to get proof against them anyway."

Now that I knew the whole picture, all I had to do was make sure the good guys won.

"You're going to publish the documents?" I asked.

"Yes."

After a half an hour of steep climbing I began feeling hungry. "Let's take a break," I said.

"Okay, good. But please take a look at Grusha. Her wounds look more infected."

After a snack of nuts and dried fruit, I called Grusha over, but I knew what I would find. The cuts were worse. I put some more salve on them, and antibiotic powder on her sausage.

"If this doesn't work, we'll have to take her to a vet when we leave the mountains," I said. I gave the dog a couple of pats on the head.

"Nick, I see how you care for Grusha, how you risked your life to save her, how many times you have to carry her. You are a bad man, but I'm beginning to like you. Grusha is a consolation to me."

"We'd better get moving," I said. It was all very nice, but I remembered that even Hitler had loved dogs and roses. I gave her another fat piece of sausage. I had plans for Grusha and wanted her healthy enough to walk.

When we started up the mountain Katrina gave me a friendly pat on the ass. Women's lib had come to exotic Yugoslavia.

We changed leads after a few minutes. This last mountain was more massive and tougher than anything we had met yet. I was covered with sweat but felt good. Those long, hot soaks the night before had done their work.

We pushed higher and higher. There was nothing to do but put one foot in front of the other and not think about the rest. Katrina was in good physical shape, but she had to stop more and more frequently. The undergrowth of shrubs and trees was especially thick and troublesome.

We saw no wildlife except a couple of wild boar near a stream. They paid us little attention as they thirstily drank the cool, refreshing mountain water. Within half an hour we had reached the cliff below the end of the valley and collapsed on the ground for a badly needed rest. I looked up at the cliff. It was about fifty feet high. I could climb it without rope, but I didn't think Katrina could, and of course Grusha and the packs would have to be hauled up. As I examined the cliff, it looked to me as if we could walk right up if we went another couple hundred yards and then doubled back along a crevice.

"It doesn't look like a bad cliff," Katrina said.

"This one is harder than it looks. Most of them are easier," I began to explain.

"It doesn't look so hard," she said stubbornly.

"No," I said, "that's the point. It's deceptive-looking and tricky." I looked it over again. "I can do it easily, but you, for example. . ."

"I can climb it."

"It's a bad cliff to learn on. But it doesn't matter, because we can walk up if we go down to those trees."

"Ah, Jesse James, you're getting lazy. You don't want to pull Grusha and the packs. I climb it, no problem."

"Why scale the cliff when we can go around and save some energy?"

"You go your way, I'll go mine." She slung the rope over her shoulder, put on her pack, and began to climb. I called to her:

"Take off your pack." She got mad but set the pack down. Then she started off again.

I knew what she was thinking—she was in great physical shape, a professional dancer, flexible, strong, with good balance. She was right about all that. There were a lot of cliffs she could scale with just that self-confidence. But the cliff in front of me wasn't one. She lacked one important prerequisite —experience.

"That's a tricky piece of rock," I said, giving unsought advice. "It will be easy to take the wrong approach. Make sure you can get out of any move before you make it." I suppose I could have forced her to go the easy way, but this way she was bound to get a lesson worth ten I could hand out. I got some dried apricots out of my pack and watched the drama unfold.

She did pretty well. I could see she was being cautious despite the bravado. About thirty feet up she made her first mistake. Then she got frightened and made her second mistake—she was hugging the cliff. One thing you don't do is lie flat against a cliff; your center of gravity should be over your feet at all times. "Trust your boots," they were always telling us. One more mistake and she would end up at the bottom of the cliff.

I could understand why she had selected the approach she did, but no experienced climber would have taken it. Nevertheless, I wasn't going to make a move until she asked for help. I watched her hunt for holds with her hands, still afraid of leaning out from the cliff and thereby making her position more secure. Now she was spread-eagled against a curtain of rock, this time hugging it for all she was worth. I could see her strain. I looked at my watch. I had to judge carefully, or she might fall. I didn't want that.

"Need some help?" I asked finally.

Silence. But I think she was crying. She didn't really want to die.

"You're only thirty feet up," I said. "You might survive the fall."

"Son-of-a-bitch!" she spoke through clenched teeth. She appeared to be gearing her strength for one more, very chancy move. It would have been chancy even for an experienced climber. She was certainly stubborn.

"Don't do it, Katrina."

"I'm going to fall," she said, not moving a muscle.

I began climbing the rock face, figuring that was as close as she'd get to asking for help. It was pretty easy until I got about six feet away. I stopped to get my breath.

"Do you know what a jam is?" I asked.

"No."

"If you made a fist, would it hold onto anything?"

"No."

"Can you reach into a crevice, a crack, anything? Then spread your hand."

"I don't know, I don't know," she said.

I edged my way up a bit further, digging my fingertips into two thin crevices and wedging my right heel against a tiny knob of rock. I couldn't move next to her without risking getting as stuck as she was—the rock was too smooth. I moved around a bit, and finally saw a possible route. I had to hurry.

"Katrina, I need the rope," I said when I was near her again, but now I was on the other side of her. I slipped my foot under the rope and slowly edged it up her arm.

"Listen, Katrina, you're going to have to be very brave. Lift your right hand long enough for me to slip the rope past. First move your left hand two inches to the left. Feel the crack?"

"Yes."

"Carefully slip your hand into it. No, wedge your hand in." When she was steady I yanked the rope. For a second she lost her balance. I could see her lean back from the cliff, but she caught herself. I began to worry. It appeared she was weakening. There was only one thing left to do.

"It looks to me like you're going to fall before I rescue you, Katrina." She said nothing, so I figured she was too tired to get mad. But I had to get her mad. Anger brings strength and Katrina needed a lot of it at the moment. I started by insulting her, making sure every word I uttered hit home. Then I insulted her father. Her face began to turn red and her eyes flashed at me. Then came the ultimate insult; I attacked her country and ridiculed her countrymen. That did it.

"Son-of-a-bitch," she said between clenched teeth. She was shaking. Now all I had to do was channel her anger into energy.

"I'm surprised you're still holding on. I thought you'd be at the bottom by now," I said as I rapeled down to her level and swung over behind her. It was a somewhat intimate embrace. I tied the rope around her.

"Okay, let loose." But she didn't. I'm not sure whether she couldn't or wouldn't, but I had to kick her feet out from her. She fell away from the cliff. Then I released one end of the rope, and she went up as I went down. When she reached the top she hung there unmoving for a few minutes before she was able to get herself together enough to push herself up over the ledge.

It took me awhile to get Grusha and the packs up. Then I climbed up, rope-free, like a monkey. She was lying on the grass, crying. She looked at me with big, hurt eyes.

"You almost got yourself killed with that stunt and ruined the mission in the process," I said. "One thing you learn as a professional, Katrina, is that the work is dangerous enough without taking unnecessary chances."

"I really thought I could climb it. I was very careful."

"We all make mistakes."

"Why did you insult me and say all those horrible things?" she asked as she got her things together.

"I had to get you mad."

"You said them to make me mad? But why?"

"Katrina, you were afraid to move an inch. I had to make sure you'd move or you would have fallen.

Your anger gave you the strength and the presence of mind to get over that ledge." She stopped and thought about this for a moment. Then she looked up at me almost shyly.

"Thank you," she said softly. "Thank you for me and for Grusha." With that she got up and hoisted her pack on her back and stood waiting for me. I wasn't sure but I think that meant that we were on good terms again. With Katrina, one never knew.

For a time we walked along in silence. But it wasn't too long before Katrina said, "We're almost there. It's just through those trees.

We continued through the rest of the forest and came out into a clearing.

CHAPTER XIV

In the middle of the clearing a dozen Bogomil tombs were basking in the afternoon sunlight. From the clearing I could see the outline of the valley for the first time. The cliffs were high and steep. The peaks of several mountains were barely visible above them. I understood why both the Bogomils and the Nazis had chosen this spot. There was ample water in the stream that ran along the far side of the valley. The cliffs, while presenting little problem to small numbers of men familiar with them, were a formidable obstacle to a large force trying to capture the valley. The peaks, if trails were cut into them, would provide a three-hundred-and-sixty-degree view of the surrounding terrain.

"I'd better have a look around," I said to Katrina. I left her in the clearing while I looked around the valley. I could find no evidence of where the German outpost had been, but I found deeply weathered stone steps at the base of the cliff, which I suspected had been cut by the Bogomils six hundred years before.

It seemed ironic that Nazis who were here thirty years ago had left no visible trace, while Bogomil handiwork was evident everywhere.

I walked back to the clearing. Katrina was consulting her maps and pacing off distances. I watched as she finished the last of her work and stood in front of a flat-topped tomb. Grusha was running around happily. Her infection seemed better for the moment. Looking at Katrina bent over examining the tomb brought to me a sudden desire I couldn't ignore. I walked up behind her, and she turned and gave me a friendly smile.

"I'm glad we finally made it," she said. "This is it." She pointed to the tomb. "They must be buried in the tomb." Buried documents was not exactly what was on my mind.

"Nick, you're looking at me funny. Are you all right?" I looked at the tomb meaningfully.

She looked at the tomb, too. "What are you thinking," she asked as I slipped my arm around her and pressed her against me.

"Oh, not now." She kissed me. "Tonight, Nick." She kissed me again and pressed against me surprisingly hard.

"We must do our duty first," she said. I unbuttoned her blouse.

"Oh, Nick, not now. Tonight." I undid her bra, exposing her full, beautiful breasts.

"Oh, Nick, no." I took her breasts in my hands and kissed her neck. We swayed back and forth. I reached down and undid her belt. "Nick, no," she said, but her taut, yielding body was sending another message.

"Nick, are you serious—right here?" She glanced at the tomb. I unzipped her pants and rubbed the smooth skin of her belly.

"Nick, what if those shepherds see us?"

"We're going to violate the tomb anyway, right?

This way we'll die happy." I slipped down her pants and bent down and kissed her stomach. She shuddered.

"Oh, Nick, it will be cold." I slipped her panties down around her ankles and leaned her back on the tomb.

"It will be warm," I said, quickly stripping off my clothes.

"Oh, Nick, you are so beautiful."

"You are more beautiful," I said as I stretched out on the tomb beside her. She took me in her hand while I reached down and touched her. She sighed and relaxed. I nudged her gently over onto her stomach and she responded willingly. I massaged her back slowly, all the while marveling at the satiny smoothness of her skin. She purred like a cat and arched her back. I took this opportunity to reach underneath her and stroke her magnificent breasts. Again she moaned.

"Oh, Nick," she breathed. "Please, don't stop."

I had no intention of stopping. We were both overwhelmed by the pleasure we were deriving from each other's bodies. I reached around her belly and brought her back up against my stomach. She writhed up and around, the whole of her back rubbing the length of my torso. We both quivered in mutual delight. Then suddenly she beckoned me with her lovely bottom. I eagerly complied. Ever so gently I pushed her head and shoulders down so that she was at a more acute angle. There before me were two golden globes glistening in the sunlight. I placed both of my hands on the curve of her hips and pulled myself into her. She gasped at the suddenness of it. Then slowly she caught on, picking up my rhythm. We moved as one, unaware of our immediate surroundings, savoring the perfection of the moment. Then, as if by some unspoken signal, we started moving with an increased urgency, each wanting to satisfy the other's need. We worked ourselves into a frenzy, and at the moment when I thought I couldn't stand it any longer, a thousand lights seemed to burst in my head sending ripples of pleasure throughout my body. Katrina let out a long, heavy sigh, her body trembling beneath me. I gently kissed her behind each ear. She rolled over on her side and smiled at me. Then she leaned over to kiss me on the nose and then the mouth. With that she lay her head down and drifted off. I followed a moment later.

When I woke up hours later, Katrina was sitting at the end of the tomb tickling the backs of my knees with a blade of grass. I leaped for her beautiful, naked body, but she slipped out of my grasp and put on her panties.

"No more of this fooling around. It is time we found the documents. Besides, there will be more time for that later." She smiled provocatively as she pointed to the tomb. She was right; there'd be time later. I walked over to take a look at it. The top was a single, seven-and-one-half-foot slab of stone, dusty-orange in color. I squatted down to take a closer look at how the top was fitted to the rest of the tomb. The sides came down, overlapping the base about four inches. I walked over to one end. I got myself in position to lift it. I checked my grip, took a few breaths, and pulled. Nothing! I bent down and took another look. I figured I just hadn't pulled hard enough. I couldn't see that it was locked in any way.

I returned to my post and pulled. For a second

nothing happened. Then the massive stone rose up. Humid, earthy-smelling air escaped. I moved the slab sideways, changing my grip when necessary, until it slid down beside the tomb. Then I took a look. I expected to see either the papers or a box, but instead there were only rocks and dirt. I turned to Katrina.

"You're sure this is the right place?"

"Yes, of course. You think I'm an idiot?" I just looked at her.

"I'm sure it's just under those rocks and dirt," she said.

"Yeah, but how deep?" I sighed and walked over to her. "I want to check the map before I dig this whole thing up." She gave me the map. She was right; this was the spot.

"Get the cooking stuff," I said.

"Why don't we eat after we dig, mister lazy bones." I went over to the gear and dumped it on the ground. I searched through it until I found a shallow metal pot. Then I went to the nearest bunch of trees and found the exact size branch and in five minutes had a sturdy, makeshift shovel.

When I got back to the tomb I shooed Katrina away. "One at a time," I said. "Why don't you get us some dinner?" Then I went to work. I suspected that if they had gone to the trouble to bury it, they had buried it a long way down. An hour later I was still shoveling hard and knew my hunch had been right. Katrina brought over some soup. I sat on the grass while she began digging.

"Why don't you put on some clothes?" she said, looking me over.

"I'm going to the stream first."

"Nick, Grusha has been acting nervous."

"Okay," I said, "I'll take a look around when I return." I watched the dog a minute and then went to bathe. I took Wilhelmina along. I watched the cliff while I splashed around in the icy water but saw nothing. I went back and dressed and got my binoculars.

It was already dusk as I climbed toward the base of the southern cliff. I found what looked to me like another ancient trail, faint and overgrown. Soon I found what seemed to be a trail that was cut into the ancient rock. I climbed for a quarter mile, until I reached a place blocked by a slide. I took out my binoculars and for a long time studied the rough terrain, the cliffs themselves, the mountain peaks, and what I could see of the valleys. Then I went back to where Katrina was digging. I watched her for a while. She looked beautiful, even digging up a tomb.

"What are you looking at, Jesse James? I have no OZNA in my pants. Why don't you come dig?"

"In a while," I replied. I wanted to take a look down the end of the valley. I always make sure there is a way out, and when I'm worried, I make sure there are two ways. I wanted to see if the path we had argued about was there and useable. When I emerged from the trees at the edge of the cliff, I stopped to survey the valley below. I searched carefully but saw no signs of life except the thin smoke of a distant campfire.

I worked my way to the left, looking for the path I had guessed was there. It didn't take me long to find it. I followed it quite a way down the hillside. It was very passable because it had been heavily used to haul supplies by both Bogomils and Nazis. It was also in use as a deer trail; there were dozens of deer prints everywhere. I was pleased.

When I got back, Katrina was still digging and sweat was glistening on her forehead despite the cool night air.

"Help," she said.

"In a minute. I want to set up my camera."

"Anything to get out of work. There's not enough light. You have to wait until tomorrow."

"It has a flash," I said as I went to get the camera and set it up. It looked like an ordinary 35mm single lense reflex camera. But of course it wasn't. And the document stand doesn't look like a document stand until it's unfolded and joined to a piece of the camera case. The film I use is a little hard to develop and I get a hundred and twenty shots to the roll.

"Nick, I'm tired, and it's getting dark," Katrina said, panting.

"Okay," I said. "I'll take over."

"Look at Grusha, will you?" she said as she climbed out of the tomb. I called Grusha over and had a look. Her wounds were infected again despite everything we had done. I hoped she would make the rest of the trip. I kept my thoughts from Katrina.

"Better take her down to the stream when you go to wash off. Clean the sounds again," I said. I went over and took the shovel from Katrina. She kissed me on the cheek; she was covered with perspiration. I looked over our progress. We were already about four-and-a-half feet down. I wondered if they had broken through the bottom of the tomb and buried it still deeper. I began shoveling. Once I got the rhythm I began digging faster and faster. I took off my shirt. I was seven feet down when I heard my makeshift shovel scrape metal. Five minutes later the metal box containing the papers was sitting on the ground beside the tomb. The tomb had been a smart idea. It protected the box and papers as if they had been in a dry cave.

The box was padlocked, so I smashed it open with a rock. Katrina pulled out the oil-paper packages. I pulled out a similar-looking package and pulled at the wrapper. Out poured thousands of Deutsche marks from the World War II period. I watched Katrina go through the papers.

"This is it," she said. "What we hoped for, but there's so much material here. It's the reports of the controlled ones' activity. I don't see names. . . . Ah, yes, okay. This man is now head of the air force." She was excited.

"You know," I said, "the most secure thing would be to photograph the material and rebury it. That way they would never know you had it until it was published."

"No. I want the real documents. It will help us. But do photograph them."

"Select the most important papers. I've only got two-hundred-and-forty shots and you've got what looks like five or six hundred pages."

I spent the next hour photographing the pages she handed me. I was sure we had gotten everything we needed.

"There were eight of them to begin with," she said. "I don't know whether to be surprised at how many there were or how few. One died during the war. Another is the man who confessed to the Fox. A third is Deijer. He is the head of one of the republics. They rotate; for short periods he will head the country. He is the only one we knew about. A fourth man, Tokaravic—I don't know who he is. Maybe he is dead. Anyway, he never amounted to much."

"He might be in OZNA, so his name wouldn't be known," I interrupted.

She nodded distractedly. "There is Duplja, head of the air force; Blatopek, the second secretary of the party; Sulzavic, an ex-ambassador to the U.S. That must have been handy for them. He is the number three man in the foreign office now. And last but not least is Iz Rapavic, head of OZNA." She looked at me meaningfully. The last revelation had particularly upset her.

"You knew it was going to be bad news, so there it is," I said. "Each man will have had time to plant dozens of agents within his respective organization. How long has Rapavic been the head of OZNA?"

"Why, he is head now," she said.

"It makes all the difference in the world. Until he got very high up, it would have been hard to penetrate an intelligence organization, even if he got a man inside. Then it becomes easy. Your father will understand these things. But as a practical matter, every day that he has been in charge lessens your chances of success."

"I understand what you're saying; I'm not stupid. He became head of OZNA some time last year."

"Probably a lot of OZNA is still loyal to the Fox. He can count on only certain sections of the organization in his fight with you."

She regarded me curiously. But I could see I was becoming more and more useful in her eyes and not just brawn. When we finished photographing the papers I tossed the empty box in the tomb and slid the lid back on. It wouldn't fool anybody, but it was worth a try.

"We should move out first thing in the morning —not even have breakfast," I said.

"Yes, I agree with you. I'll wrap the papers and put them into my pack. You'll have to carry some of my things and we have to decide what to leave here.

It took us about an hour to work out the details. When that was done, I called Grusha over. She had really grown to trust me. I got out my backpacking scissors and trimmed the hair under each of her forelegs.

"What are you doing?" Katrina asked. I took out special adhesive patches. "I'm taping the film cannisters under her legs. It won't hurt her. I've put these same patches on my own legs."

"Let me see," she said, leaning over. "You let me bring Grusha just for this, didn't you? If we were searched or lost the pack, we'd still have film of the documents."

"There were a number of considerations." I looked at her. "I like the dog, you know that, but you didn't ask me if you could bring her for sentimental reasons. You asked if it was in the interest of our mission."

"You're a cold one, Jesse James."

"Maybe, but it's your country at stake. Come, Grusha," I said, "let's go for a walk." Wagging her tail, she was only too happy to go off for a walk with me. The western sky was a deep purple stripe, but the rest of the sky was darkening except where a bright yellow full moon shone. I watched the dog, but there was none of the nervousness she had evinced earlier. The wind, which had been coming from the east, had shifted to the west and was now rushing uphill in gusts.

I wasn't sure what kind of reception I'd get when I returned to camp, but I noticed the sleeping bags had been zipped together. I stripped. Katrina was naked in the sleeping bag.

"You feel warm," I said.

"And you are so cold," she returned. We snuggled close to let the heat of our bodies warm us. The warmth turned into a fire that consumed us both. We came together fervently, our bodies melting into one another. Neither of us uttered a sound until we reached the peak of our excitement, and even then all that could be heard were sighs of content. Our fire turned slowly to embers as we fell into a heavy sleep.

CHAPTER XV

I awakened from a deep sleep to Grusha's whining. It was a clear night; the stars shone brilliantly. The moon hovered low in the west like a dying spotlight. I could smell the fir trees in the cold, moist air and hear the stream bubbling a hundred yards away. It was hard to believe that anything could be wrong at this moment. I called Grusha over, put my fingers near the infected claw marks, and pressed the cannisters to see if they were rubbing her. I got no response, and this worried me. Grusha continued whining. My senses are extremely sharp, but still I heard nothing. I reached for Wilhelmina and then sent my other hand searching for the heavy flashlight just as I heard a twig snap.

I knelt in firing position, Wilhelmina in my right hand, the flashlight in my left. I stared into the darkness. Grusha was growing more agitated. I reached over and shook Katrina lightly and pressed the back of my left hand to her mouth.

"What are you doing?" she whispered.

"Shh. Get your gun," I whispered back. She looked around quickly and crawled over to her pack. She looked beautiful, naked, in the moonlight. She came up next to me, gun in hand.

"What is it?"

"Dress quietly." I listened and thought I heard another twig snap. She came back wearing her jeans. I reached down and slipped on my shirt. Grusha lifted her head higher, sniffing the wind. I stood absolutely still, listening, but now I heard nothing. Grusha was growing more nervous.

"Hurry!" I whispered.

I gestured toward the tomb and reached for my pants. Grusha started to growl low and menacingly. Katrina hadn't moved. I gestured again, then slipped on my shoes. She started walking; every step betrayed our hiding place. I reached back and took her by the arm.

"Move quietly. Get your pack and get behind the tomb." She looked worried. Still keeping my eyes in front of me, I edged over to my pack. I reached in hurriedly and fumbled around for my extra clips and ammunition, my passport and money. I threw the camera and case as far as I could. Grusha's growling grew louder. I knelt and covered Katrina. I heard distinctive sounds now; they were quick and light. I started moving back myself. I don't know what I expected—wolves? Katrina had mentioned them. It sounded like a pack coming toward us. Grusha was crouched low and began barking loudly.

I could see shadows rushing us, darker than the night around them. They loomed larger and larger, dark as death, all teeth, all speed. I switched on the flash. Dobermans! I aimed for the lead dog and fired. I felt Wilhelmina's solid push against my hand. It reassured me, but I have never faced more difficult targets in my life. The dog did not drop on the first shot, so I fired again. Its howl splintered the night; blood spurted everywhere.

There were four more. I couldn't get them all, but I stayed steady and chose my target. Just then Grusha charged past me and grabbed one by the throat. The point dog was sprinting for me, not barking, not whining, just running—silent death. Wilhelmina's third shot blew the dog's head away. I blasted the third dog out of the air as it leaped for me at point-blank range. The teeth of the fifth dog clapped around my gun hand.

Wilhelmina dropped. I could feel pain and warm, sticky stuff over my hand. I brought the heavy flash down again and again on the savage dog's skull, until it cracked open like a walnut. There was more sticky stuff flowing in the dog's final spasm. I pried my hand loose. Grusha was losing her battle; her infection was tapping her strength. I picked up Wilhelmina, shined the flashlight on the writhing, twisting dogs, and moved closer to get a better aim. I picked my shot as carefully as I could, barely three feet away, and squeezed the trigger. The doberman flipped into the air. Grusha ripped away at the throat of the fallen dog. I could hear Katrina firing rapidly. I wondered what she was firing at. Suddenly I was on the receiving end of a burst of light. The ground around me exploded with automatic rifle fire. I pulled Grusha off the fallen doberman and dragged her back. The ground was churning with destruction, and pieces of dirt and rock splattered all over me.

I sprinted across the campsite and jumped, landing on my stomach behind the tomb. Katrina's little automatic spoke again and again. There was another burst of automatic rifle fire from the unknown enemy. The tomb sounded like an unwholesomely plucked piano as the bullets squashed and richocheted off of it.

"My gun is empty," Katrina said. Her eyes flickered questioningly.

"We'll make it," I said. I reached up and let Wilhelmina roar at the moving shadows and flickering lights. Automatic fire shredded the ground in front of the tomb. But this time I saw the rifleman. Wilhelmina sent him a couple of kisses. When I heard him grunt I put a slug into the ground where I thought he'd fallen. I didn't want to take any more chances with automatic rifle fire. But just then a second automatic opened. I shot it out with him one on one.

I kept low as I took my aim at the second rifleman. I let my shot go and it reached home; I heard the dull thud as the second man went down. I slipped to the ground to put a new clip in the overheated luger. Katrina emptied her gun. It seemed to me that only a couple were still returning fire.

"More are coming," she said. "I can see their flashlights all over the mountain." I saw a dozen fragile beams cutting through the darkness.

"It's useless. Move back toward the cliff," I said. "There is a path down on the left. I'll cover you. And take the light."

"Grusha," she called out. Grusha padded over and Katrina took the blood-soaked dog in her arms. I shined the light into the field looking for any wounded. I didn't want to get shot in the back as we pulled out. But not one man was alive.

I saw Katrina running with the pack slung over her shoulder and Grusha at her heels. Then I heard the sound I least wanted to hear: barking. I heard men shouting back and forth. I moved back through the field of tombs, catching fire from a single shooter. I cleared the tombs and ran straight for the trees. The forest was pitch black. I could hear the barking of the dobermans getting closer.

"Nick, Nick," I heard suddenly. It was Katrina.

"Run," I said. "As fast as you can."

In a few minutes we emerged on the lip of the cliff. If there hadn't been moonlight, we would have gone over the edge. We had the flashlight off so they wouldn't see us. We circled to the left. I couldn't find the trail, and it sounded as if our pursuers were still getting closer. "Turn on the flashlight for a second," I said.

"There's the trail," she said.

I gave poor, confused Grusha a shove down it. I could hear Katrina thrashing her way down the path ahead of me. Then there was a strange moment of stillness before I heard the dogs and men again. I slipped a fresh clip into Wilhelmina and waited while Katrina went ahead. The seconds seemed like hours. Then I heard scraping feet. Lean, black shadows leaped from the woods. There were five dogs this time. But the two leaders were unable to stop in time and bounded right over the cliff. I blasted the next dog broadside.

The last two charged, all teeth and muscle, and I opened up. Concussions and the stench of powder filled my head. Hugo flicked into my left hand. The first dog fell but the last leaped for my throat. I was knocked off my feet and my shot went wild. I protected my throat with Wilhelmina. Only one of us was going to get up, I knew. There was a second when I thought I had come to the end of my journey, but Hugo hit home, deeply. I twisted hard. I pushed the still-kicking corpse aside and stood up, but there was no respite. Men had arrived, and I heard another pack of dogs in the distance. My bullets scattered among the trees and the emerging men. One man screamed, then another. Suddenly I was drawing a great deal of fire. There was only one automatic rifleman; I was lucky. He died when he stepped out of the trees. I had excellent cover among the boulders, and if my luck held out, it was going to cost them dearly to take those rocks.

I emptied Wilhelmina and dropped down to put in a new clip. I had bagged only one more. My shots splintered more wood than men. They were being more careful, taking more precise shots at me. I knew my tide was going out. It was time to move on. I kept down until I was sure they had left the trees and were moving up on my position. Then I popped up. I got three with the first three shots. They scuttled for cover. I nailed one in the back of the shoulder. They'd take these rocks on their bellies or wait for reinforcements before they tried again. Then I turned and ran. Every second would count now as I tore down the mountainside half blind. I went crashing through branches in the thickening woods, jumping over rocks.

When I thought I'd gotten far enough ahead of them I yelled Katrina's name, but I got no response. I yelled again. Finally I heard her voice, far off, but I could see nothing.

"Nick, Nick," came the voice again. I tried to pick up speed; it was a mistake. My foot caught a root and I was thrown forward, stretched by my own momentum like a string. I gasped for breath. It was a minute or two before I could move in spite of the inconsequential nature of the injury. Then I searched among the rough roots for Wilhelmina. When I found her I raced off, having lost precious time. I could hear the dogs barking, and when I looked back I could see flickering lights in the distance.

"Here!" came a loud whisper.

"Katrina."

"Here!" it came again. I caught her in my arms. It felt good to touch solid flesh again.

The night was filled with ghost-black trees and death, and the dogs were getting closer. We ran through the woods, but the dogs were almost on us by the time we reached the next clearing. I turned and opened fire. I caught one of the black shadows sideways. The other four bounded for us growling. Wilhelmina barked and blew a dog's shoulder away. But now even as I stood firing I knew I had no chance. I could get one more, but the other two would be upon me before I could shoot them. Again Grusha sprang out from behind me and bounded for the lead doberman. The second raced past me and leaped at Katrina, who fired at it. I shot the third between the eyes as it leaped for me. I twisted and ran to Katrina. I don't think I've ever moved faster. I jumped on the dog as it pushed in for Katrina's throat and smashed it to the ground with my own weight. Then I ripped and slashed with Hugo until it drowned in its own blood. I saw the doberman rip poor Grusha open as if it had a knife instead of teeth. I grabbed the doberman by its collar and swung it round and round into a tree until its spine snapped. I went over to Katrina, who was kneeling by the wounded Grusha. A short burst of light from Katrina's flashlight told me the dog had been fatally wounded.

"Get away," I said to Katrina. "Get back." I had to put Grusha out of her misery. I plunged Hugo into her heart and cut away the cannisters from her legs.

"We must get to the stream," I said.

And again we were running. Katrina stopped and turned back toward the fallen dog. I took her by the shoulder and pushed her forward. We ran down an incline to a small stream. Soon we were splashing along in the cold water, tripping and bumping into rocks and logs. The cold stream seemed to run colder and colder as we ran. We saw lights and heard more dogs, but it was over. We had escaped, at least for the moment.

"I'm freezing," said Katrina. "I can't feel my feet anymore."

"We won't have to stick to the stream much longer," I said. I looked up and through the trees and saw the first faint signs of dawn. I had a crucial decision to make—move west or to the north. I chose north, but didn't tell Katrina. Within an hour and a half we had reached the thermal springs.

"I don't understand," she said when she realized where we were.

"We wouldn't have made it the other way. They'll keep west. This is the logical way for us to go. We need a chance to rest and figure out what to do."

"Nick, I'm so cold and tired." We were both shaking with the cold by the time we spread out our clothes to dry and immersed ourselves in the steaming pools. We lay in the water a long time without speaking. I kept my shoulder out of the water most of the time. I had gotten a bad bite. But from time to time I immersed it so it would bleed clean as the hot water opened the wounds.

We found a patch of warm, filtered sunlight and stretched out on the smooth, warm rocks and slept. Two hours later we were back in the pool.

"I lost the pack, I don't even know where," Katrina said. "You were right to photograph the documents." She looked at me. "You do have them, don't you?"

I nodded. "They might even be our luck—the photographs, that is. They may believe they recovered all the documents and give up the chase. I threw the camera as far as I could when the shooting started."

"We have lost everything."

"We have the film and our guns, which is all we'll need." That's what I said, but I wasn't as sure as I sounded. "What are our plans from here?" I asked.

She said we were to head east, where a car was to be left for us at the end of a dirt road. But that meant going back toward where we had been attacked.

"I have an uncle who lives south and west of here about sixty miles," she said. "He is a lifelong party member, but to Montenegrans like us, blood is thicker than water—I hope. I think we should go there. It will take us two days to hike to the nearest road."

"Do you have ammunition?" I asked.

"A little. I have one candy bar and money, but I lost my passport. The matches are wet and my clothes are practically in shreds." She laughed a little.

"They look fine to me," I said. "I have my money, gun, both passports, and my matches in a waterproof container, but we can't set any fires anyway. And I have a small bag of peanuts. Why don't we have dinner?"

"Shouldn't we save them?"

"We're going to get hungry, whatever we do. It's better not to have false hopes. You can't get un-hungry on what we have, anyway."

"Maybe we can shoot animals," she offered.

"That's for storybooks. We can't fire the guns. The energy you expend isn't worth the trouble un-less you get lucky. We'll fast. It won't hurt us."

"We won't starve?"

"No. Not in two days. We'll just have to be care-ful. And you might get a little skinny." I gave her a big smile. I was surprised when she smiled back. But her smile quickly turned to a frown.

"Someone betrayed us."

"Here, have some peanuts," I said.

"We were betrayed."

"Maybe, maybe not. Don't jump to conclusions. It could have been an accident. A code could have been broken or someone had luck. Sometimes you never find out. Did Ivo know where we were going?"

"He would never betray us."

"Torture, drugs. They can break anyone. Here," I said, "have some more nuts."

"I don't want peanuts."

"Yes, you do. I can tell. You're hungry."

"You must be hungry, too." I splashed across and poured the last of the peanuts out of the bag and into her mouth.

"I thought you wanted me to be skinny."

"You'll be skinny," I said.

"Do I look too terrible?"

"You couldn't go to a debutante ball in that out-fit." She did look a mess, bruised and cut. She also looked beautiful. I slid between her outstretched legs and we made love.

CHAPTER XVI

I lay in the warm sun feeling as if I were a part of the rock I was lying on. I knew it was time to go, because the air was beginning to cool. But when I got to my feet, I felt like I had been hit with a thousand hangovers. I began to regret breathing, much less moving. There was nothing to do but walk over and stand under the icy waterfall. Katrina came over and joined me.

"Do you feel terrible?" she asked.

"Sure," I said. "I'm human."

"Let's stay the night."

"No, we've got to go. We have to cross the mountain range tonight when it's dark."

She didn't say anything, but after she had dried off she went over and put on her clothes. Women dressing have always seemed magical to me. I checked Wilhelmina and my extra clips. I had twenty-five slugs left. That was not good news, but I expected worse. Katrina approached me, hands on hips.

"I want the cannisters," she said. "They're my responsibility." I paused a second but handed them over to her. She gave one back to me. "In case something happens to me . . . Okay. I'm ready," she said. She was a real trooper. We headed down the hill. After a while I began feeling better, but I knew we would soon begin climbing again. First we had to cross the same valley we had been chased down the night before. I expected this to be the most dangerous part of the day's trip. But when we reached the valley it had a fairy-tale peacefulness to it.

I studied the thick woods carefully but saw no sign of the violent struggle that had taken place the night before. Soon we reached the cliff. It was more formidable than I had expected, but in a way that was good. It would seem a less likely route to take.

"Do exactly what I do," I told Katrina. "Put your feet exactly where I put mine. This is no time to be creative."

"I think of Grusha," she said, gesturing to the valley where Grusha had died.

"These things happen," I said. I looked up at the cliff. "One thing, Katrina. Don't look down."

We climbed the cliff in silence. I was struck by how tired I got. I was already hungry. Although my efficiency would drop because of the lack of food, once my body adjusted to using stored energy the decline would stop, at least for a couple of days. I caught a glimpse of the mountains we would have to climb before we headed downhill. I hoped they weren't as bad as they looked.

We made fair time the next two hours. It was dusk when we threw ourselves in a thick bunch of bushes to rest. I set the alarm on my watch for ten o'clock that night and was asleep almost the instant I closed my eyes. When the alarm went off, it was dark but the moon and starlight provided enough light to see the mountain range. I woke Katrina.

"Oh, Nick, I feel as if I was drugged."

"Come on," I said. "We have a mountain to climb."

"I can't do it. Let's wait until tomorrow." I pulled her to her feet.

"You'll only feel worse tomorrow. You can have a nice long nap when we get to the other side."

"I am so very tired, Nick." But that was the end of the protests. Soon she was walking along behind me at a steady pace. I suspected it would be an easier climb than the one we had made earlier in the day, but much longer.

We felt our way up the mountainside. The moon cast strange shadows through the tall trees and everything was distorted. It was hard to tell a shadow of a branch from a real one. We didn't dare use our flashlight. When the moon slipped behind an occasional cloud there was nothing to do but wait for it to return. The night grew eerie. We heard strange noises, animals moving in the brush or calling to one another. We were very tired; it was all we could do to put one foot in front of the other. We struggled up, higher and higher. The forest thinned and shortened, finally becoming nothing more than stunted shrubs, a moonlit version of the now-familiar pattern.

A few minutes later we climbed out into a barren world of moonlit rock. I felt oddly elated as we made our way over the pass through the empty, haunted landscape. Once I thought I saw the glow of cigarettes, later a cough and the sound of metal rubbing. But as we climbed over the pass and then down into the valley the basic silence seemed to deepen awesomely. I was so tired I scarcely cared what happened. My mind became a little confused from the night and the strain. I began to miss having Grusha with us. In my confusion I imagined her still padding along with us like a friendly ghost.

When we reached the first of the large trees we pushed our way into a thick clump of bushes for protection and warmth and collapsed arm in arm. We fell asleep instantly. I was so exhausted I forgot to set my watch alarm, but my internal clock woke me at exactly nine o'clock the next morning. I was hungry and still tired but pleased with our progress, even though I knew we'd have to make a similar trek that day.

All morning we hiked through the thickly forested valley without speaking. We were very hungry. My mind wandered but always came back to the message my stomach was sending.

"Nick, I'm so very hungry." Kartrina finally said.

"We'll make it out of here today, Katrina. You'll sit down to a big dinner tonight." I sounded sure, but I knew we had another mountain we had to climb. When we reached the base it was only noon. Katrina and I decided to go ahead and climb it and not wait for dark.

When we had been climbing an hour, I angled over away from the lowest pass onto a higher, steeper route. I figured we were less likely to find it occupied by our friends from CRML and OZNA. Minutes later we had climbed to the edge of the forest. I slipped out and lay among the stunted trees and rocks studying the pass but saw no sign of the enemy.

When I went back into the forest I found Katrina asleep. I watched her for a minute and noted the peaceful expression on her face. I hated to wake her, but we had to move on. Soon we were gingerly threading our way through a boulder field. I kept a sharp eye out for trouble and even dusted our clothes with dirt to make us less visible from a distance. Finally we stood a hundred yards below the bare, rocky pass. There were high, jagged cliffs on either side and no real cover below in the pass we'd have to walk through. I didn't like the look of the place, but we didn't have another choice. We groped our way up the rocky talus slope to the path between the two pinnacles. I motioned to Katrina when we reached the top and pulled out Wilhelmina. She pulled out her pistol, too, but I still saw no sign of our friends.

We edged along, hugging the left-hand cliff about twenty feet apart. I searched above us each time before we moved. We walked cautiously but quickly because there was little cover. After about a hundred yards we reached the other side, where the pass opened out. We could continue to hug the left cliff, but I wasn't sure we could get down without a rope, because the path appeared to end abruptly at the edge of the precipice. To our right the trail edged around a large, rounded talus slope. The valley stretched out far below us. There were a few steamer-trunk-size boulders but otherwise no cover for about two hundred yards. Then the trail dropped off, following a steep, rocky stream into the woods below.

I searched the cliff above and saw no one. I jogged out along the trail about a hundred feet and looked back up at the cliff. Nothing. I waved to Katrina to follow. We had gone another thirty feet when someone opened up on us. I dived for some rocks and looked around. Katrina was beside me.

"Damn! I was so careful," I said.

"Don't blame yourself."

"Damn!" I stuck my head up for a look and felt a bullet whistle by. A single sniper with a high-powered rifle was on the opposite cliff. They hadn't thought we'd try to cross here, so they'd stationed only one sentry. We were safe as long as we didn't move. Sooner or later, though, he'd be joined by his friends. We weren't that far from the safety of where the trail dropped, yet neither of us had a chance of making it across that small distance alive.

The son-of-a-bitch was clever. He'd let us move far enough so that we were out of effective pistol range but still well within that of his rifle. I reached up with Wilhelmina and took a couple of careful shots at him to test out the obvious. I raised little dust holes in the cliff, but that was it. Next he edged out to a more exposed position and blew holes in the ground around us.

Katrina fired a couple of shots his way, but her little automatic had about half the effective range of Wilhelmina.

"Now what?" she asked.

"I'm not sure," I said. I lay in the dust trying to think, while the sniper tried getting us with ricochets. I decided he wasn't a good shot, otherwise we'd have been dead already. That's when I remembered Waldo. Now, if I followed orders strictly I'd wait until I was sure there was no hope, hold Waldo up to my face, and erase permanently all evidence that I had been in Yugoslavia. I had no intention of using Waldo on myself. I had other plans. I reached down and unzipped my pants. Katrina looked at me in disbelief.

"Waldo," I said in answer to her look of outrage.

"Oh," she breathed in obvious relief. I showed her the little corrugated bomb.

"Can you throw it that far?" she asked.

"Probably not." I was looking around for something to make a sling with. You can heave a rock three or four times as far as you can throw it and as many times as hard with a sling. I undid my shoelaces. I was looking around and saw what I needed. I told Katrina to take off her pants and give me her panties. She turned a light shade of red but knew I wasn't fooling around. Quietly she did as I asked. I looked around for a rock as close to Waldo's size and shape as possible. I would use Katrina's panties to nestle Waldo in.

I worked hurriedly to finish the sling. I handed Katrina Wilhelmina. "You're going to draw his fire. But don't stay in one place long. Shoot so you look convincing. Don't take time to aim." I gave her a stern look. I wanted her to be very serious. This whole business was going to be tricky.

"Okay," I said. She looked serious. I gave her a sign and spiraled up to my feet, whirling the stone over my head. He pumped a couple of shots her way before he realized I was a better target. By then I was diving for the ground. Still, it was close; rocks were splintering all over the ground when I landed. I scurried for better cover and popped my head up to look at my throw. I had missed the cliff. That meant I would have to try again.

"He almost shot me," Katrina said. There was blood on her cheek. I reached over and touched it.

"Just a piece of rock," I said. "We're going to have to do it again. Do you think you can handle it?"

"Yes," she said. "But please be careful. You nearly got hit before."

We shifted positions and tried it again. I spiraled to my right and up. Katrina was up and shooting, and I was swinging my sling. I took more time this try, even though I left myself wide open for him.

This release felt right. I dropped backwards to the ground. He pumped his shots in front of me, and I slipped around to watch my second practice shot. It dropped on the cliff about ten feet below him. If that had been the real McCoy, he'd have been dead. I looked at Waldo. The only thing that worried me was how long Waldo's fuse was set for. Not long, I guessed, figuring what Waldo was designed for. I smiled to myself. Our friend was in for the surprise of his life.

"Listen, Katrina. Same kind of thing as before. Only, when you hear the explosion, run for it. Don't look back. Nothing that might happen here will make any difference."

"I'm going to take a couple of shots before I start moving," Katrina said. I watched her carefully; the timing had to be right. She slid across the ground quickly and came up on the other side of the rock from which she had been shooting before and began pumping Wilhelmina's bullets at him. I spiraled up and whipped the sling round and round my head. Out of the corner of my eye I saw Katrina grab her chest and flop to the ground, writhing like a hooked worm. I swore I'd throw Waldo down the son-of-a-bitch's throat. I took a couple of more wind-ups, let Waldo go, and dropped to the ground. I looked over at Katrina.

She gave me a wink and said, "Pretty good actressing, no?"

"Get ready to run," I said. There was a deep

concussion. I looked up at the cliff. A big piece was missing. Waldo must have dropped right in his lap.

We rounded the mountain and then climbed a hundred yards down a boulder-strewn stream before stopping. She grabbed me and gave me a big hug.

"You're some fighter, Jesse James." She kissed me again. I thought we weren't going to make it. But you aimed Waldo perfectly." She was beaming.

"Don't forget that you helped," I said. I undid the sling and tossed her the remains of her panties. Then I took the shoelaces and strung them back in my shoes.

"They'll know exactly where we are now, won't they?" she said.

I nodded and finished tying my boots.

CHAPTER XVII

We were tired and battered, but things had become simple. We had only one task before us—run. Nothing else mattered, not the pain, not the mission, not the fate of poor Grusha, not even the constant hunger. I looked over at a weary Katrina laying against a tree, still panting from the exertion, and hoped she understood this. I knew we should rest for an hour, but we couldn't stop here. We had to get as far from the site of the ex-sniper as quickly as possible.

"Come on, let's go," I said.

"Oh, Nick, I'm so tired and hungry. How much more?"

"I wish I knew. Come on." I got up and offered her my hand. She pulled herself to her feet and we started down the mountainside.

"At least there'll be no more mountains to climb," I said.

"We'll be out of the forest soon and into the karst country. It's as wild and rugged as this, but there will be no large forests to protect us," she said.

I'd been in the karst country before, but even so it always seemed strange and unnatural. The karst

165

is a deeply eroded highland of chalky limestone. Water does strange things to it. There are deep gorges, sink holes, caverns, rivers that run above ground and then dive into rock, not emerging for miles. The chalky stone makes poor soil, so there are only tiny patches of fertile ground and small clumps of trees. The rest is wild, barren, and as picturesque as anyone could want. Unfortunately, I didn't want picturesque; I wanted safe and secure.

If I were our pursuers, I'd wait at the edge of the karst country, where the forest thins, and try to pick us off there rather than waste time trying to find us in the vast expanse of trees.

We jogged as fast as we could through the deep forest.

"Nick, I can't go on without rest."

"Okay, an hour," I said. I set my watch and collapsed next to her. I woke up promptly when the alarm went off, but it wasn't so easy getting Katrina going. Two hours later we were nearing the edge of the karst country.

"Katrina, I said no more mountains, but we're going to have to climb this little hill here so that we can move along the ridgeline. They'll expect us to be tired and hungry and take the line of least resistance moving along the valleys."

"It's more like a mountain," she said wearily. I had to admit it was tall for a hill, but it wasn't nearly as high as the mountains we had climbed earlier. Eventually we made it to the top.

We edged our way cautiously along the ridgeline as it gradually sloped into karst country. I wished half a dozen times that I had my binoculars, but I didn't, and with the naked eye I saw no sign of our pursuers.

We followed the ridge down until it almost reached the level of the plain. Before us was a great, deeply etched plateau of karst. I studied the landscape uneasily until I saw a small canyon running south and west that looked like our best shot. We climbed down from the rocky ledge and slipped into the small defile. At first it was not deep—only a few feet above our heads, but soon it emptied into a larger gorge and that gorge into another still larger. The small, green streamlet cutting down in the center canyon had become a gray-green torrent rushing like a mountain stream after spring thaw. For the moment it seemed safe. The canyon continued to deepen and soon we were walking between two-hundred-foot-high, gray-white walls, half rock, half chalky talus. We kept up a good pace. Once established, the rhythm seemed to carry us along despite our bodies' aching protests.

We moved down a long, particularly straight section of canyon. When the canyon began to angle off to the right I turned around abruptly. It was the oldest, simplest trick in the book. I saw figures moving along both sides of the canyon's rim about a quarter of a mile behind us and knew we were in serious trouble. I pointed them out to Katrina but hurried her along. We picked up our pace and began putting some distance between us and the pursuers. At first this made me hopeful, but after a while I got suspicious. They seemed so confident; they were apparently in no hurry to catch up, and I began to wonder if they knew something we didn't.

I kept looking up at the cliffs. There were few boulders, little cover of any kind, and the canyon walls were steep and crumbly, the worst combination. There were several spots where we could have climbed to the rim, but in the open we would be at an even greater disadvantage carrying only our pistols.

"They have sent some men down to the canyon," Katrina said.

"Yeah, I know. We're in a tough spot."

"We will make a fight of it, Jesse James. That, I promise you. What comes, comes. I just hope they attack us before I'm too tired to hold my pistol."

We had to slow down some because Katrina couldn't maintain the pace. I didn't push her. We could lose them in darkness, but spring days are long. All they needed was rifles and it wouldn't be much of a fight, despite Katrina's brave talk. I patted her on the ass; I couldn't think of anything else to do.

"You like that, huh, Jesse James?"

"Well enough."

"I am so hungry I could eat a caraboose."

"What's a caraboose?"

"You know, like you have in America. Great big deers with funny horns. Carabooses."

"Yeah," I said. "I could eat one too."

"When you go back to America, you order a caraboose steak in remembrance of our escape."

"I'll order two, one in remembrance of you. I know a great diner in Buffalo. Caraboose steak is their specialty."

They were closing on us, but slowly. I hoped they were just overconfident. But when we rounded the next bend I was genuinely surprised. I shook my head, thinking I was seeing some kind of mirage. The entire roaring green river disappeared into a giant sink-hole in the limestone cliff. I knew such geological features existed—the karst country is famous for them—but I couldn't believe we had stumbled onto this one. Quite simply, we were trapped. I sat down on a boulder, trying to decide what our next move would be. We were exhausted, low on ammunition, and a dozen well-armed and well-trained men were moving in on us. It was hours before dark. I looked around us at the high cliffs of loose, chalky talus. It really didn't look like we had much of a chance. It would be a long, slow climb, and they would be here before we made it. Either that or they'd be waiting for us on top.

I looked at the disappearing river and rested my head in my hands. I sat there for several minutes. Katrina sat next to me and threw her arm around me. I guess she was too tired to say anything. I looked around but my eyes kept on coming back to the rushing river. Suddenly I had an idea. What goes up must come down—what goes under must come up. I looked at the river with new eyes. This would be our way out.

"Come on, Katrina," I said. "We're going for a swim." She looked at me strangely but didn't protest.

"This river comes up out of rock in about a hundred yards," I continued. "Hopefully we will, too."

"But some run underground for miles," Katrina said with worry.

"Let's hope this isn't one of them." She shuddered visibly.

"Okay, here's how we do it," I said. "First, a little playacting to make it look good. We pretend to climb the cliff. They shoot at us. We shoot back and fall into the river. The tricky part is not actually getting shot." I turned and looked behind me.

They were obviously moving into position. There was a man with a rifle on the far rim of the cliff. His buddies would be here soon.

"Okay," I said. I strapped my belt around the palm of her hand and wrapped the free end several times around mine. "Stay very close. Try to stay right behind me just under my legs. Take your left arm and wrap it around your head. The only real danger is being knocked out onto the rocks."

"Nick, this is crazy. We cannot do this."

"Come on," I said. "This is our only chance." I pulled her along toward the loose, sloping cliff. "One thing, Katrina. It might be a little longer than a hundred yards. If you feel air and we're still underneath, breathe deeply—and quickly." I watched the roaring river vanish between limestone jaws.

. "Nick, I don't agree with this, I—" she said, but her last word was lost when they opened fire. The chalky ground began puffing around us. She was staring at the water, her wide blue eyes filling with terror. I turned her head away.

"It's like climbing on the cliff," I said. "Don't look. Take it one step at a time."

"Aren't you going to kiss me goodbye?"

"No," I said, "absolutely not. You're not going anywhere except for a swim." They opened fire again. I fired back, then did my stumbling act. We slid on the crumbling rock and dropped toward the river.

The shock of the icy water brought home terrible doubts about my plan. The green-white water looked a dull, plain gray now that we were in it. The roar grew louder. I looked up through swirling water at the dirty limestone cliff and the black cavern, which seemed to be reaching out for us rather than waiting for us to be swept in. The sudden horror of dying in the darkness, trapped underground, made my guts knot up. The maul grew larger and larger. The sound of the cavern grew not only louder but hollower as we neared it, like some immense animal moaning. I took one last deep breath as the water swirled around us and swallowed us up bringing us into absolute darkness.

I kept my eyes open but saw nothing. I fought to keep us in the center of the swirling stream. I felt a slashing pain as my arm cracked into the ceiling. We tumbled in the roaring water. But my mind was completely clear, as if I were in a clean, white room watching the whole event while sitting quietly with a martini in my hand.

The absolute dark continued and was punctuated with abrupt, blindly felt stabs of pain. I kept my head protected as I had told Katrina to do. We smashed into walls, protruding rocks, and I don't know what else. Darkness, darkness every direction. My thoughts were becoming confused. I felt the pressure under the jaw that comes with suffocation. My lungs began to ache. I could see no light. Past, present, future, daydreams, nightmares, everything was becoming confused. I was running out of air. Katrina must have been too.

I fought my way up to the top and ran my outstretched hand along the ceiling. My brain was like ticker tape, reading the news my hands sent. Water, water, water, air. I pushed my head up, searching for the air, only to be smashed against rock. I slid deeper into the gushing stream but fought my way up again. Again the outstretched hand sent messages. Water, water, water, air. I pushed my head up and sucked in a breath. Never have I felt anything so good in my life. I kicked Katrina, signaling her to breathe. Then I actually got a second full breath before my outstretched hands felt rock coming and we dived back into the center of the icy torrent.

The blackness went on and on. Pain struck me like the pop-up monsters in a fun house—when I least expected it. The familiar pattern of oxygen starvation reasserted itself in the throat, the jaw, the lungs. We tried to surface again, but my hands just got slashed. My chest began to burn. My brainwork got confused. I thought huge, terrible faces were watching me die. Nick Carter and friend were about to join the great majority. I began losing consciousness but refused to suck in water.

Then I saw light. It took seconds for the meaning of light to register. When it did, I pushed to the surface and breathed in deeply. When my head cleared, I turned to Katrina, who was coughing desperately. I swatted her on the back and started pulling her to shore. Soon we were lying on warm rocks, battered but alive. Katrina had a smile on her face, but her eyes were closed and she hadn't spoken.

"Okay, let's go," she suddenly said and she opened her eyes.

I laughed. "*Now* we can rest a few minutes."

"Will the film be all right?" she asked.

"It would take a hand grenade to puncture those cannisters," I said.

The combination of relief and exhaustion made it hard to get moving. We followed the canyon another mile and climbed up on a rugged, rocky plateau. Soon we were dropping into thick forest again.

"How long do you think the cavern was?" Katrina asked.

"I don't know. But we may be safer now than we have been so far. Not only will they think we're dead but also that they've recovered the documents. If I were them I'd pull all my people out of here in order not to attract any more attention. The best thing is to let the corpses turn up in the natural course of things."

"They won't follow us?"

"They may get suspicious if our bodies don't turn up in a week or so."

We said little more. Eventually we came to a dirt road, which we followed from a distance of a hundred yards into the woods. The first mile we saw nothing but a few birds. Ahead was a small clearing. Just then Katrina grabbed my hand and pulled me back. There was a picnic basket in a patch of moss, and a couple lying on a red-and-white-checked tablecloth. Two naked, blond-haired bodies.

"They must have a car near here," I said. "Let's take a look." It didn't take long to find it, parked just off the road. I looked it over. It was locked. There was nothing unusual about it except it looked like there were rice grains or confetti on the back seat. I didn't want to steal the car unless I had to, because I didn't want any mysterious incidents reported to the police.

"Let's give them a few minutes," I said. We sat down heavily on some rocks and waited. "We'll tell them a sob story, and convince them to give us a ride to your uncle's."

We didn't have long to wait. They came up, arm in arm, happy as a pair of porpoises. We popped up and Katrina began a long, involved sob story. I watched their faces. They reacted with real concern. I was sure we looked an absolute mess. They wanted to take us to the hospital. We told them we just wanted to go home. There was some confusion when Katrina started to explain we were German-speaking Swiss tourists on our honeymoon. I noticed the Swiss license plates just in time. I gave her a little kick and interjected that we were Yugoslav. Katrina looked at me evilly, until they explained *they* were German-speaking Swiss tourists on *their* honeymoon.

Pretty soon we were bundled up in sweaters and pants that they insisted we put on. It felt good to be in warm clothes in the back seat of a car. They offered us the remains of their lunch, which we ate gratefully. The couple chatted away, and it wasn't too long before we made it to the dusty track leading to Katrina's uncle's farm. We insisted they let us off there and gave them our thanks and said goodbye. Finally we headed down the road toward the farm.

CHAPTER XVIII

The burst of energy we had gotten from the first food in days and the realization that we had actually survived didn't last long. Soon it was all we could do to lift one foot after the other as we walked down the dusty road. The scenery was pretty—shining yellow fields, groves of pale olive trees. The driveway looked even less promising than the rutted track we had been walking along, but the modest white farmhouse looked like just what we needed. Katrina left me and went up to the front door. She came back a moment later with a smile on her face. I was looking around the place when Katrina suddenly leaped up in the air laughing and shouting.

"Well, Nick, it looks like we have the farm to ourselves for a couple of days. My uncle was called away on business and left a note for his farmhands to stay away until he returns. She searched under an old flower pot for a key. Her enthusiasm for the place was unlimited. "Look," she said, "running water. Look, flush toilet. Look, electricity." By Western standards the place looked pretty modest, but by Yugo standards it was quite a place. She had just sat down in a big easy chair to show me

how comfortable it was, when she closed her eyes,
yawned, and fell right asleep. I carried her to the
bed.

The next two days were the best of the trip.
There was plenty of food, a lot of quiet, hot show-
ers, a comfortable place to sleep, and Katrina. But
the best always ends, and a quick two days later we
left, hiking over a low range of mountains down to
the highway. We hitched a ride to the small Bos-
nian town of Belicia, where I figured we were far
away enough from the scene of our last encounter
to chance stealing a car. Katrina disapproved, but
I said we'd leave money stuffed in the back seat as
compensation. She finally admitted there was no
other option.

We drove the stolen car to the little Serbian town
of Doboj and bought train tickets to Vinkobi,
which was actually out of the way. At Vinkobi we
changed our clothes and rode separately to Ljubljana, the capital of Slovenia, a hundred miles past
Zagreb. We passed our real destination for a purpose. I was determined to weave a complicated pattern that would take CRML and their infiltrants
into OZNA weeks to untangle. We went shopping
in Ljubljana and then rented a car.

The whole complicated business had taken a day
and a half, and it was almost noon when we finally
pulled into Zagreb. Katrina had calls to make, so
we stopped across from a booth on one of Zagreb's
broad, tree-lined boulevards. The city is much better preserved than Belgrade but lacks the latter's
exotic oriental touch. The Turks never quite
reached this far north and east, when their great
Ottoman empire spread over much of the Balkans.

I watched Katrina's expression shift. After some

calls she looked happy, after others disturbed and worried. She came over to the car in the middle of one call.

"What kind of ammunition do you need?" she asked. She still didn't like the idea of getting it for me. When she had finished her calls she walked back to the car looking the best she had in days. I admired her legs; they reminded me of the frightened but self-possessed woman I'd first seen walking over to my table at the café in Belgrade. I was getting used to her and liking it.

"I think I have found a safe place to stay, Nick." I nodded.

"I should explain something about the situation here," she said. She looked solemn. "I don't know how much you know about Croatian politics."

"I know a lot, but how do they figure in with the documents and CRML?"

"The Croats are a proud people who for a long time have been dominated by others. There are feelings of independence here. Croatian nationalism somehow took a bad turn. Many welcomed the Nazis until most realized they had made a mistake. The Fox is Croat and always kept them in line. But there has been a violent separatist movement here for some time.

"Some want a small, independent Croatian state. It would be easy pickings for our Eastern cousins. Blood of Croatians is now the worst group. There may be trouble. Many of the people who will help us are Croatian dissidents who oppose the Blood.

"A few weeks ago they distributed some pamphlets showing that one of the Blood's leaders was responsible for killing many Croats during World

War II. This has hurt the Blood badly, even with extreme nationalists. The Blood is angry and is trying to get even with the Croatian dissidents. There have been attacks on my friends, and the police do not stop them. We will have not only CRML and their OZNA infiltrants to deal with but also these fascists. I am sorry about this. I would not involve us in all this except I have no other place to turn. These are the people who will help us expose the controlled ones."

"You're going to publish the documents here?" I asked.

"Here and elsewhere. We'll publish them here in Zagreb and also in Belgrade and in Skopje, the capital of Macedonia. The Macedonian president is a controlled one. I plan to stay here until everything is published and then go to Belgrade to see my father. A courier is to come from Belgrade and one from Skopje to pick up the photographs of the documents.

"Once we have duplicates of the film and things are set, I want you to leave the country and take the duplicate film to the West—in case something happens to us. Promise me, though, that you won't publish the material before us."

"I promise. I think our government will honor it, but sometimes when national interest is at stake, pressures can be complicated." She patted me on the knee and gave me her friend's address.

"Oh, Nick," she sighed. "I will be so glad when this is over and I can go back to making dances again."

She said her name was Silvie. She took my hand so gently that I barely knew she was touching it.

She was tall and thin and had big black eyes and shining black hair. Her arms and legs were slender, her breasts large for her body type, and she looked as delicate as a bird's egg. Her skin was white and translucent like bone china. She said she was a dancer like Katrina but with a different company. We would be staying with her for a couple of days.

"Say very little to the dissidents," Katrina had warned me on the way over. "Don't lie about school or a job; they will just check you out. They will ask friends of friends of friends until they find someone who knows you, or worse, someone who should know you and doesn't. It is better to be mysterious. I will vouch for you. You speak our language so well I don't think they will suspect."

"Right," I said. When Silvie told me what she did, I told her nothing in return. Once she and Katrina had started talking, I took a look around the apartment. It was on the third floor, and there were two exits. I leaned out a window and noticed an overhanging roof three stories up. The weakest part of the apartment was the doors and locks. I gave Silvie some money to buy locks. I figured I'd pick up some wood and a couple of iron bars myself. Katrina went to make calls. I sat looking at Silvie, and she sat looking at me. Such big black eyes ought to be illegal. Before we got around to talking, Katrina came back in the room.

"Nick, we have a delivery to make. Silvie, I won't be back until very late, but Nick may be back sooner."

A minute later we were out in the street.

Katrina said, "Let's walk. We're going to the photographer's who will develop the film. He helped publish the pamphlet that angered the

Blood. His office was attacked and he sounds shaky. Please stay until you have the duplicate film and then bring it back and hide it at Silvie's. I have many errands to do."

We climbed four flights of stairs in a prewar building much like Silvie's but in worse shape. Katrina knocked on the door and said her name. There was no immediate response. Katrina explained to the silent door once more who she was.

We heard what sounded like furniture being moved. Shortly thereafter the door opened a crack.

"Milos, it's Katrina."

"I know, I know," said the small man with glasses as he emerged from behind the door. "I am sorry. The Blood broke up my shop. I'm a photographer, not a street fighter. I'm against those fascists, but I'm not made for this. My assistant quit. She had been with me for years." He looked at me. "Who is this man?"

"A friend, Milos. Now calm yourself." We walked into a narrow hallway to the living room. A table leg was wrapped in tape sitting on a table.

"Expecting company?" I said.

"I . . . I hope not," he said. I helped him slide some furniture down the hallway to block the door.

"You know, three people have been badly beaten," he said. "Two are still in the hospital." He spoke nervously.

"So we have heard," Katrina said. "Your shop was totally destroyed?"

"Yes, but I have always done most of my developing here. You've got film for me?"

I handed him the cannisters.

"This has to do with the Blood?" he said.

"No," I said. "With CRML."

"Our country has always had more than one enemy," he said. "On one side are the fascists, on the other the Stalinists like CRML." He tried to open the cannisters but couldn't. I reached over and showed him how.

He looked at them nervously.

"I want to talk to you privately, Katrina," he said. He hurried her into a nearby room. As he closed the door I heard him say nervously, "What is this, Katrina? These are not ordinary cannisters." I moved away from the door to have a look around. The place would be a trap if there were ever an attack. When they emerged from the room, he looked more sheepish and worried than ever.

"Nick, I must go," Katrina said. "You say the film is tricky to develop. Please help Milos for me."

He had trouble developing the film. It was designed to be impossible to develop unless you knew the exact specifications, but even when you knew them it took much effort. When he put the film in his enlarger and saw its incredible resolution he got upset all over again. He began to complain how difficult it would be to blow it up and make prints and so forth. I was getting tired of his griping, so I opened up my wallet and started counting out money on the enlarging table.

"How much equipment do you figure you lost?" I asked. "We want to help you out." I kept counting. His frown turned to a grin.

"I would do this for nothing," he said, "but I have expenses. I am not a rich man."

"I understand," I said and took out my wallet again to give him more money.

"Enough, enough!" he said. "I really don't care about the money. I will donate it to the cause."

I nodded and put away the wallet. It might be for the cause, but for all I knew maybe he just wanted a demonstration of our ability to protect him.

When he finished duplicating the negatives, he asked, "Can you get me out of the country?"

"The borders are pretty open," I said. "Rent a car and drive, *after* you develop the film."

"I thought maybe you could help me get a job in the West."

"I've never been out of Yugoslavia in my life."

"I am sorry. I should know better than. . ."

"Nonsense," I said magnanimously. "Ask me anything you want. There are no secrets here." I gave him a broad smile and he scurried back to work.

It took him a long time to duplicate the film; it can't be done the normal way. I stayed in the darkroom with him until he had finished. I slipped the duplicate negatives into my pocket. He walked me to the door, where I showed him how to wedge it shut properly. It was dark when I left the building, but the air was refreshing after hours of sniffing chemicals. I detoured over to the main shopping street and picked up some materials to reinforce the door.

I knocked on Silvie's door even though I had a key. She opened it looking more vulnerable than ever in a yellow bathrobe, fresh from the shower. I went to work on the door. The locks she'd gotten weren't much, but they were better than the others. I put the metal and wood reinforcement bars in place and then painted the whole thing with white paint. It looked very civilized.

Silvie came over while I was finishing up. "I like the door," she said. "You're a good craftsman." I smiled. She was fragile and beautiful, but somehow Katrina was on my mind and I could only admire Silvie—but that's as far as it went. I think she understood that, because her next words were, "Katrina is very lucky." Again I smiled.

When I finished with the lock, I went into the bathroom for a much-needed shower. When I came out, I found Silvie and Katrina sitting on the single worn green sofa, sobbing. Newspapers were spread around.

"Ivo is dead," Katrina said, bursting into sobs again.

I walked over and picked up the papers. SCULPTOR KILLED IN AUTO ACCIDENT, read the big headline. I scanned the article; it all sounded suspicious.

Silvie had stopped sobbing a little.

"Why don't we try to eat dinner," I said. Silvie offered to make us something and went into the kitchen. I sat down beside Katrina and opened the paper. There was a long obituary and pictures. He was a famous sculptor. The photographs did him justice: Ivo standing with his arm draped over one of his big sculptures, Ivo receiving the Lenin prize, Ivo in his judo outfit, Ivo riding a motorcycle and waving. I leaned back and started reading the article.

Katrina began sobbing again. "He was such a good man," she said.

"I know. But he should have left the country when we told him to. By the way," I added, "if you don't get some protection for Milos, he is going to end up as dead as Ivo. That place of his is a death-trap." Just then Silvie came to the door.

I got up and walked into the kitchen and attempted dinner. Katrina couldn't eat. Silvie sat with me but ate nothing. After a while I heard Katrina make some calls.

I was leaning back in my chair looking through the paper after dinner when Katrina walked in. "I want to see the film," she said.

"It's under the floorboards in the bedroom." She didn't look herself, so I went and got the film for her. Her eyes were bright red, but she looked through the film with a magnifying glass.

Abruptly she said, "There will be a meeting tomorrow night, so please be there. Would you do me a favor and stay with Milos tomorrow, then bring back the prints when he's finished? But be careful. More people were attacked by the Blood today." I watched her. She was really hurting, but she forced herself to stay together. I liked that.

"Then the day after tomorrow you can take the duplicate film out of the country. Make your preparations. You remember our agreement."

"Yes," I answered. "I can come back if you need help."

"I don't think that will be necessary, thank you." She went and made some more calls.

That night we all slept separately. For some reason Katrina preferred it that way. When I woke up the next morning, she had already gone. It looked like we were back where we started from.

CHAPTER XIX

"I'm going to make a call," I said to Silvie as I slipped Wilhelmina into her holster and headed for the door. "See you tonight."

"There's a phone here, Nick."

"Not for this kind of call there isn't." The big, bedroom eyes watched me leave.

It was a nice, brisk morning. I walked almost a mile before I picked a phone booth to make my call from.

"Hello, Rosa, this is Cousin Dmitri."

"Ah, Dmitri, it's good to hear from you."

"Is that lovestruck young guy still following you around all the time?"

"No, Dmitri. I haven't seen anyone. No one even calls me, although there is nothing wrong with the telephone." Now came the hard part.

"I'm going to cut my vacation a little short, but I think I'll spend my last day in Dubrovnik. Why not join me?"

"Yes, Dmitri."

"I remember when we used to go hunting as kids, Rosa. Most of the girls were afraid of guns, but you were always such a good shot. And you didn't have to come with us."

"It's been a long time, Dmitri. I used to like tagging along behind you just to make sure nothing happened to my little cousin while he did his errands."

"Yes. They are going to be staging a Western play—Shakespeare's *Coriolanus*. Why don't we see that?"

"I'd like that, Dmitri." She paused. "Dmitri, I remember how much you always liked to play with toy boats and planes when we were children."

"Boats more than planes, Rosa, especially toy submarines."

"Ah, yes, I remember how you used to have them arranged."

"Here is the recipe my mother wanted you to have. Got a pad and pencil?" I gave her the coded message for Hawk.

"I'll bake it up myself tonight," she said. We went through the rest of the double talk. I was glad to hear she'd be on the evening plane to the AXE station in Italy. I hung up the phone, thinking of black, lacy underwear.

I didn't like asking for her help. Protecting somebody's back is an easy way to die. But I couldn't take any chances getting the film out.

I waltzed over to Milos's place at a leisurely pace. But when I got there, I received a rude awakening. A goon was standing across the street who looked like he'd make a good tackle for the Steelers. I hurried up the steps.

After a good five minutes of arguing, I finally convinced them to open the door. Milos's normally pale face looked ghostly, as if Death himself had put on make-up. There were three men with clubs in the living room and a shotgun was lying on the table. I pointed out the goon across the street.

"We see him," one of the men said. "He's been there about an hour. He's a Blood. We've met before."

Milos hustled me off to the darkroom to see the prints. I flipped through the glossy black-and-whites. Some of the documents were in German, some in Serbo-Croatian. All, I suppose you could say, were written in treason. Men who betray are least likely to have scruples, yet when I read between the lines I couldn't help feeling some sympathy. These men squirmed like worms trying to get off the hook. There was a litany of excuses, explanations about why this or that piece of information had been wrong or was not available.

Still, they had almost succeeded in destroying the Fox and crippling the partisan army. The Nazis had launched a surprise attack on the Fox's headquarters with a special paratroop battalion and almost killed the Fox and his entire staff. The Fox had forgiven many things, but that attack had nearly cost him the war. It certainly had cost him many friends and colleagues; he would never forgive it. So the Nazis' controlled ones had become CRML controlled ones until there was a stack of betrayals a mile high.

"How much longer?" I asked Milos.

"I was up all night. Another hour and I'll have them all."

"Good. Once you're finished I think you should go away for a while." Milos wore his usual worried expression. I patted him on the back and walked back into the living room.

The men were young and strong, but they didn't look much like fighters to me. They told me that the Blood had been hitting their people for quite awhile, but that nobody had been killed although more of their friends were in hospitals from an attack overnight. We watched the street from the window. I had walked away to rest my eyes a bit, when they called me over. A van pulled up and half a dozen tough-looking men piled out. Then a green Zastava 100 pulled up and out poured more thugs. They were carrying clubs, chains, and sledgehammers.

"Maybe we'd better get out of here," said one of the younger men.

"Milos isn't through developing the prints," I said by way of saying no to them.

"We wouldn't make it anyway," said another.

"Then we'll have to make a stand," said the tough blond who seemed to be their leader.

A minute later the door started splintering. I pulled out Wilhelmina.

"Wait," said the leader. "Neither side has used guns yet." I looked over at the shotgun. He followed my eye.

"Only as a last resort," he said. I put away Wilhelmina and picked myself a club from a batch on a chair. When the fascists finished off the door they began shouting: *"Blood of Croatia is shed for freedom"* over and over. The effect was kind of nasty.

They piled into the narrow hallway, knocking and shoving the furniture back into the living room. They screamed, *"Death to the betrayers of nationhood!"* as they came at us. But I noticed some hesitation when they saw us standing ready to fight. They hadn't expected to meet four armed men. They had expected to bust up a single, meek little photographer. I noticed something else, too, something that would cost them dearly. They were packed so tightly in the narrow hallway that they wouldn't be able to fight without bashing each other. If we stopped at the doorway, we could stop them. They might outnumber us three to one, but they would never have more than two guys fighting at any one time.

The room exploded in screams. We attacked. I went for them swinging my club like a Neanderthal and shouted for effect. I smashed into the goons head on, while the rest of our guys moved in to support me. Some bones got broken. I was faster and more unpredictable than they were, and the Blood paid for it.

Pretty soon three of their guys were spread out on the floor. They had no room to maneuver. I waded into them, bringing my club down over and over with everything I had. I had to let down my guard in the process, but they were getting hurt too badly and too fast to take advantage of it. The dissidents pulled one of the Blood into the room and worked him over. Another guy dropped to his knees. I brought the club down, screaming like a banshee. When I couldn't get through his defense I kicked him under the jaw. I kept waiting for the Blood to break. For a while I thought they would just keep coming until we had finished them. Finally, they broke. It was a massacre. Only two escaped. It was unlikely that they would be back.

The victory was particularly vicious, I think, because it was the dissidents' first, after taking a lot of beatings. I went to get Milos, because we had to leave in case they did decide to return with reinforcements. I didn't rush him unnecessarily, though. I let him get his things together. I kept the set of prints to be published in Zagreb and gave the other two to the blond guy to give directly to Katrina. When I came back the dissidents were standing around the fallen Blood looking sick, their triumphant bravado dissipated. What had seemed only a vicious game to them was now over; two Blood were dead. I wondered if the dissidents had the heart for this kind of savagery. The Blood would take man for man as payment, and the dissidents knew it. The hallway was filled with groans and cries of pain; the walls and floors were splattered with blood.

One of the younger men began to sob. I slapped his face hard, then pushed him along the hall with the rest.

"I've lived here twenty years," Milos said. "I'll never be able to come back."

"Let's hope you'll be able to leave," I said. When we got outside, the bullets began flying. The blond guy opened up with the shotgun, and I pumped some slugs their way with Wilhelmina. There were only a couple of them left, and as soon as we returned the fire they ran for it.

"I don't know what's happening," Milos said. "I'm a peaceful man. I haven't been in a fight since I was a boy." He stopped to look back the way we had come.

"Keep moving," I said.

"My whole life. Everything is gone."

"It's the only way," I said.

"But where will I go?"

"I've got a place you can stay tonight," I said. I took him to Silvie's.

She was very nice to him. I hid my set of prints under the bedroom floor. Then I checked

Wilhelmina and told them to keep the door locked and went to the war conference Katrina had told me to attend that night.

Eight of them were seated around a long wooden table and another four or five scattered about the room. I spotted Katrina on the other side of the room. I could hear people moving and talking in the other rooms. Half-empty cups of Turkish coffee were everywhere. I recognized the men I had fought against the Blood with. The introductions seemed to go on and on, but all I remember was Andrej, the tough blond. When I was seated, Andrej continued to press home some point he had been trying to make.

"For the first time today, we stood up to the Blood and won. We beat them and they outnumbered us three to one. They ran for their lives."

"Yes, we fought them man to man," said another one.

"It's time to smash the Blood once and for all," Andrej said. "We will defeat them. We are tired of being terrorized by these goons. We must defeat the Blood first; then we will take up the problem of CRML and Katrina's 'controlled ones,' which I grant you is just as important."

"I agree, the Blood are dangerous. We have to defend ourselves," said Katrina. "But I'm sorry we have to fight them, because CRML is the real danger to our country. They may already control the Fox's secret police, and they certainly have connections with the KGB. If the Red Army rolls into our country, it will all be over."

Andrej spoke. "Katrina has a good point. But it is the Blood who beat up our people and the Blood whose existence is a stain on our honor."

"They are insignificant," Katrina insisted.

"They are just a local group. CRML is everywhere. It's CRML who have infiltrated our government."

At this point I decided to join the debate. "I don't want to take anything away from your victory this afternoon, but the Blood's loss was an accident." I explained about the narrow hallway. I could see that my words carried some weight because of my role in the fight.

"You won a battle, but do you really want to fight it out with the Blood one on one?" I asked. I looked around the room sizing up each individual in turn. Only three or four had any muscle. I did this melodramatically, getting them to see what I saw.

"We'll use our brains," said Andrej, answering my unspoken question.

"It's a fool's errand," I said. "The Fox's men have no love of fascists. They are playing the Blood off against you. What you must do is pressure the Fox and OZNA to repress the Blood. Get out pamphlets, go to the international press and complain about fascist attacks. You'll force the Fox's hand. He'd never allow the world to believe he is soft on fascism."

Suddenly three or four people were talking at once. Katrina broke in and did some talking. They argued on and on. At that point I went into the kitchen for a glass of wine and a bite to eat.

Just when I had found myself a glass of wine and fixed a sandwich, Katrina burst into the kitchen. "Nick, it's Silvie," she screamed. "Some men are trying to break into her apartment."

We ran down the stairs. We tried to find a car or a taxi, but couldn't. It wasn't far to Silvie's. We ran all the way.

CHAPTER XX

I ran up the stairs. My heart was pounding but not from the physical exertion. I'd been around long enough to know what we would find. Still, the sight of Silvie and Milos hanging from a beam in the living room filled me with rage. At least they hadn't been tortured. Whoever had murdered them must have found Silvie on the phone and had been afraid help would arrive. I ran over and looked out the window. I saw four guys jumping into a small green car. I ran down the stairs like a madman. I ran over to the nearest car and yanked the driver out at gunpoint.

They nearly got away, but I caught up with them, almost by accident, about four blocks from the apartment. After that, following them was almost too easy. The reason was not hard to figure out—these guys were not afraid of anyone. There was nothing furtive about them, and I began to wonder if they were really Blood.

We wove our way through the darkened streets to the old warehouse district in the upper section of the city. Zagreb had once been two cities, a sacred one and a secular one, which later grew together. I had been in this area only once and wasn't sure exactly where I was. I saw the thugs pull over and park about two-thirds of the way down the block. They were laughing and slapping each other on the back as they walked over to an old brick warehouse building. There was no light on and one lit up after they entered.

I extracted Pierre. Our fascist friends were in for a little surprise. It took me a few seconds to pick the ground-floor lock. I ran up the stairs, stopping on each landing and listening at each door. On the fourth floor I heard voices below. I flattened against the wall and waited with Pierre in one hand and Wilhelmina in the other. When I stopped hearing voices I slipped down a floor and put my ear to the door but heard nothing.

I picked the lock and opened the door. There was another heavy metal door about six feet down the unlighted hallway. I left the first door closed behind me and dropped to the floor. This time I could see a faint bit of light but heard nothing much. I picked the second lock in almost total darkness.

I swung the door open. It was a large, empty room with exposed metal rafters running along the ceiling. There were only packing crates and a yellow light bulb hanging in a corner. But now I saw a light coming from under the door opposite me. This was someone's headquarters and they were reasonably professional. I looked around quickly and found an unused telephone line. I cut the cord and wrapped it double around the doorknob. I could hear them laughing. One of them said, "You should have seen her twitch. The little guy pissed in his pants when we strung him up." They all laughed. I pushed open the door. There was a roomful of surprised eyes staring at me. I smelled the booze, the stale smoke, and the fear; soon they would be sniffing Pierre. I plugged a couple of the bastards just to create confusion and tossed in Pierre. I pulled the door shut and jumped back. Bullets came splintering through the wood after me, but it was too late. I had dropped to the floor and braced myself so I could hold the door closed with the chord.

It wouldn't take long. I figured I had taken maybe ten or twelve of them. They pumped more holes in the door and yanked and pulled, but soon the sounds of anger turned to horrible cries and choking sounds. I ran across the room. I flung open the first metal door and ran down the short hallway and flung open the second. I turned and started down the stairs. Suddenly I couldn't feel anything in my right arm. There were awful-looking faces around me, and I was getting hit. I tried fighting back, but my body wouldn't listen. I felt things hitting me all over. I got dizzy, and then the world turned black.

When I woke up I found my feet and hands handcuffed together behind my back. I was lying on my stomach, and my stomach wasn't feeling so good.

"He killed *all* of them. Gas or something. He killed ten guys!" I felt a boot crunch into my ribs.

"Who are you?" I didn't say much and felt the boot again.

"You'll talk, believe me you will."

"Who is this guy?" Suddenly I was looking into a large bore gun. I saw the finger pull the trigger ever so slowly and the flash. For a second I thought it was all over, but he had moved the shot over. He was quick. My ears rung.

"He's mine," I heard a deep, grunting voice say. Soon I was looking at the voice's ugly mug. "You killed my brother," it said. He put a pen knife close to my face. "I'm going to start cutting you. Cutting off things until you die. But that's going to take a long time. First I'm going to cut off your nose." He slipped the knife close.

"Nemo, get away from him. You can have him later."

"Cut his nose first."

"No, we are going to take a ride. I don't want him bleeding like a stuck pig all over the car."

"I'm going to cut things." I could feel him fumbling with my shoe. "I'm going to save the good parts for later."

"Nemo, get away from him. You can have him after the professionals get through. I want him to spill his guts out properly."

"I'm going to cut him first." I heard the report of a pistol. Nemo backed away from me suddenly.

"Damn, you almost shot me," he said.

"You follow orders or you're going to be as dead as he is going to be."

"String him over that rafter. You guys can soften him up a bit, but I don't want a lot of blood and I don't want him dead. Understand?"

They tied rope where the handcuffs were, hauled me up in the air, and practiced high-kicking me in the stomach. Then they swung me head first into the wall. That was hard because every instinct screamed for me to put up my hands to protect myself, and of course I couldn't. When they tired of that, they hauled me up to the ceiling and let the rope loose. At the last minute they pulled the rope taut, wrenching my arms and legs back so hard I thought they would snap. Then they let me freefall all the way onto my stomach from about nine feet up. Each time I dropped, the air was knocked completely out of me and my knees banged helplessly. I tried to hold my head back from the floor, but my face slammed into it from the momentum, although not nearly so hard as the rest of me. I began thinking about my capsule. Waldo would have come in handy, of course, but at the rate they were pounding my face no one would be able to identify me anyway.

"Hey, you guys, leave some for me," Nemo said, coming over. He cut me on the neck with his penknife.

"That's enough!" I heard. "Save him for the pros."

"His face is bloody. Wipe it off." Someone pushed a dirty rag at my face.

"Hey, fellow," said the boss, kneeling next to me. "Tell me your name and I won't let them hurt you for a while."

I gave him a phony Yugo name. He scoffed at me in disbelief. "There'll come a time when you'll be begging to tell me, pal."

I lay on the floor a long time thinking.

"Let's take his fingerprints," someone suggested.

"Let's take off his fingers," Nemo said with a suppressed giggle. Suddenly I was dragged across the floor.

"Is this the guy?" the boss asked. My eyes were funny. I couldn't see much.

"Yeah, I think so. The last time I saw him was in the mountains; he fell into a river and never came out. He's got nine lives, I think."

"That was his last," a voice said.

The boss spoke again. "Let's move him; it's going to be light soon. There's no use in taking any more chances than necessary."

They pulled me to my feet and held me up. Nemo slipped past one of the guards and punched me in the solar plexus. I grunted.

"That's for my brother. Now I'm going to cut you."

"Nemo, this is my last warning," the boss said. "Next time I'm going to put a bullet in your fat carcass."

They dragged me out the doors and down the stairs. Nemo managed to slip me a couple of kidney punches as we went out. They dragged me across the street to the small green Fiat I had seen them come in and pushed me roughly into the back seat. One thug scrunched in on either side of me; the other two got in front.

"I can cut him now, huh, boys?" said Nemo.

"Show some respect, Nemo," replied the driver. "You heard the boss."

"I've always followed orders. But this guy killed my brother. Did you see him? His face was green, he was suffocating on his own puke. Have I cut anybody except under orders?" They didn't say anything.

He looked back at me. You could have cooled a blast furnace with that look.

"I'm going to fix you, fellow." He tried to jab me in the face, but the thug on my left grabbed his wrist. They started the car and pulled away from the curb, but they hadn't gone ten feet when they slammed to a halt. There was someone standing in front of the car.

"Who's that guy?" a goon asked. I still couldn't see well enough to make him out.

"There's just one guy," said the driver. "Go see what he wants." Nemo swung open his door and walked out to talk with the stranger. I squinted. He was a little, thin man with a shock of white hair and maybe a mustache.

I saw a flash and Nemo dropped to the pavement with a thud. The little man took a couple of steps casually to the left, as if he were getting ready to do a folk dance. I still didn't know who he was. A pistol hung from one end of his outstretched arm, a little lopsidedly. He looked more like a matador holding a sword than a gunman holding a gun.

I heard three light, sharp noises. He was shooting small caliber, and I understood now that he had done the dance to avoid ricochets off the windshield. Brains popped out of the back of the goons' heads splattering gray stuff and blood over the windows. I felt the guys next to me twitch and then go limp.

The stranger walked up to the car somewhat tentatively and opened the door. "Nicholas Carter, Killmaster?"

"Igor Aleksandrovich Snayper, KGB?" I answered.

I examined the small mustache and bushy eyebrows, but I had known who he was as soon as he had started shooting. We had never met professionally, since, obviously, both of us were still alive. He examined each one of his shots, muttering to himself and measuring with his thumbs how the holes were centered on their foreheads.

"Ah, I'm getting old, Nicholas. I don't shoot like I used to," he said in English with a thick Russian accent.

I coughed a little and said: "Looks pretty good to me, Igor."

"Yes, yes, well . . ." He shook his head sadly. "But where are my manners? You must be uncomfortable, Nicholas." He pulled a goon from the car and let him drop in the gutter. Then he reached in and helped me out. When he saw the handcuffs, he rummaged through his pockets until he found the key.

"Shall we walk a bit, Nicholas?"

"Wilhelmina," I said, gesturing to the car. He looked puzzled.

"My gun."

"Yes, of course." He stepped back and made ready to draw.

There aren't many rules in my profession, but an absolute one is this: One good turn deserves another. But you don't accept help from a source you don't want it from—that's what Igor thought by my wanting my gun. I was glad to be saved but less than enthusiastic about my savior. Lots of my colleagues have wound up with those neat little holes in their forehead.

I thanked him firmly for his help and very carefully slipped Wilhelmina into her holster. I could have drawn on him, of course, but then I would have been dead and my mission ruined. Igor Aleksandrovich was everybody's candidate for the finest gunman in the world.

"We should go, Nicholas." He handed me a silver hip flask. I took a couple of deep drinks—cognac!

"Not exactly a socialist drink, Igor."

"My stomach, Nicholas, is not so good for vodka."

We started down the street. He offered me his hand. I'm afraid I hobbled quite a bit. I nodded back toward the car.

"The KGB doesn't like fascists," I said.

"Those are not fascists, Nicholas. They are CRML agents pretending to be Blood, you understand?" My eyes opened the widest they'd opened in hours. He continued: "That way the Blood and the dissidents kill each other off and save CRML the trouble."

"I thought CRML and the KGB were the best of pals."

"Oh, we are, Nicholas, we are."

"Then—"

"You know, sometimes someone offers you something big—like a great dowry. All free. All you must do is marry someone called maybe CRML and bring her into your house. But if CRML comes to your house, who is to say what will happen—she already has relatives there? You are understanding, Nicholas? It takes too much guts to say no to such a fine offer like Mediterranean ports." He spread his fingers apart and held up his hand to me. "Nicholas, I have five grandchildren now. One time Uncle Joe is enough." He looked at me carefully.

"I got you, Igor," I said.

"Children I don't care so much about. Wife either. But grandchildren have walked into my heart." He looked away dreamily, but his eyes stayed crystal clear. "I am ready to retire—old man grows soft. Grandchildren grow up—no Uncle

Joe." He shook his head as he said each word firmly.

"I understand," I said. "What are a few ports in Yugoslavia compared to having CRML running the Soviet?"

"It might interfere with my retirement, Nicholas," he said sadly.

"I understand, Igor. But what can we do for you? One good turn deserves another. Perhaps something to ease retirement?" We stopped and he handed me the flask. I took a deep swallow. I was holding up my end of the conversation, but I wasn't feeling so good.

"I have good pension—and dacha—but should Uncle Joe's boys . . ."

"Four hundred thousand in a numbered Swiss bank account," I interjected.

"Two hundred thousand is enough. I'm a simple man." He paused, looking thoughtful. He was probably getting his list of requests organized in his mind.

"One son, only forty, already has heart trouble. Mayo clinic, no charge."

"Yes."

"My elder sister's son has disappeared in Argentina. I want him back."

"Ah, Igor, you know how it is down there. The innocent get chopped to pieces. Don't have hope for the guilty."

"I want my nephew."

"AXE didn't train the death squads, Igor. Someone we know did. We don't have as good connections. If they got him, he was tortured. Believe me, he is dead."

"If he is dead, very well. I want his body sent home to his mother."

"We'll do what we can, but they've got no respect for the dead down there. The corpses are scattered over the whole damn country."

"I want him buried in soil of Russia. I think you can do this for me. You tell David Hawk what would have happened to you and your mission if it had not been for Igor."

"You know us, Igor. We pay our debts." He reached into his pocket and handed me the flask again. It was almost empty, but there was enough of the hot, burning stuff to wet my parched throat. I handed him back the flask when I finished.

"Igor is retiring," he said again.

"We don't hit retirees, Igor. You know the rules. But when you retire, Igor, stay in the Soviet Union. If we see you vacationing abroad, we'll assume the worst."

"Here is CRML command post address," he suddenly said. "As you Americans say, I would get them before they get you. I'm leaving for Minsk in the afternoon."

"Thanks. I am honored to have met you Igor Aleksandrovich," I said. I looked at the world's best sharpshooter. I'd say he stood about five feet four inches if that. I started to walk away. He turned and walked in the other direction.

CHAPTER XXI

I hobbled to the cab and somehow made it to the apartment. I woke up a day later in a small white room. There was a fellow sitting in a chair opposite me with a shotgun. I looked at him, and he looked at me. I had never seen him before. He walked to the door and shouted: "He's awake."

Andrej wandered in. His arm was in a sling, his ear was bandaged, and he had a black eye. "How are you?" he asked.

"I'm okay," I said. "A bad knee and a few broken ribs. You don't look so well."

"You should see the other guys," he joked, but he was obviously hurting.

They had agreed not to do it, but after finding out about Silvie and Milos they had decided to attack the Blood's headquarters.

The Blood had been waiting for them. Seven dissidents had been killed, including one woman who was captured and raped. When they finished with her, they tossed her into a vacant lot. The police were everywhere, Andrej said. Whatever the Fox and OZNA were up to, the locals had got fed up and raided both the Blood and the dissidents. I hated to tell him it had been CRML pretending to be the Blood who had killed Silvie and Milos. He'd been tricked and had gotten all those guys killed attacking the wrong thugs.

I told him I had learned where the CRML command post was located, that they were planning a nice slaughter for him and his friends, and that we had to hit them first. I asked him how many guys he could gather.

"Yesterday a hundred, today twelve," he said sadly. He shook his head and looked unhappy. "The truth is, Nick, Katrina runs things now. I don't know whether anyone will come with me after the disaster I led them into."

"I'll take care of Katrina," I said. "A dozen will be fine. Get guns, shotguns, pistols, rifles, the heaviest stuff you can find. We'll do it tomorrow morning. I'm afraid it's the only way to undo your earlier mistakes."

"Katrina won't like it."

"I'll talk with her." I gave him a reassuring smile.

"Look," I said, "we all make mistakes. It's your pride or your life. They're going to kill you when you try to publish the papers. They'll have to. The only alternative you have is to run."

He agreed but looked far from happy. I learned that I was being credited with the neat holes in the foreheads of those guys in the car. News of it had reached the grapevine, but no one had heard about Pierre blowing his top and the consequences.

Katrina came in. "Nick, I am glad you are all right. Everyone says you have smashed CRML. But what is this I hear about more fighting tomorrow?"

I told her what had happened, leaving out the

part about Igor. I told her I had demolished the CRML imitation Blood operation but not CRML itself.

"Nick, I don't want any more violence. No one was killed until the fight you led at Milos's." I looked at her a minute and said one word: "Ivo." She gave a start at the mention of the name.

"Violence won't bring him back."

"CRML is going to kill you and all your friends unless we get them first. I argued against fighting the Blood, remember."

"I forbid another attack." When I said nothing she said, "Aren't you going to say anything?"

"The attack is on." She bit her lip. She knew there was no way to stop us.

"Listen," she said. "Pin Begovic, the number two man in OZNA, was killed yesterday in a suspicious accident. This means OZNA is eliminating the CRML infiltrators and the attack is unnecessary."

"Or," I said, "it means CRML is seizing final control over OZNA." She was so mad she got up and left without a word.

In the morning the mood was funereal. The four men Andrej had rounded up acted as if they were going to a wake instead of a shootout. They were heavily armed. I figured we'd do okay even with the small number of men. I explained what we were doing and why. They didn't look any happier.

"Look," I said. "You want to end up like Ivo Mudrac or hanging from a rafter like Silvie and Milos? Let's go."

They continued to drag their feet. "This is murder," said one.

"How do we know it's the right place?" said another. "We can't just go in and shoot people."

"If you want to wait until they start shooting," I said, "go ahead."

"But what have they done to us?"

"Okay, here's how it works," I said, and I told them as much of the story as I could.

"CRML originally infiltrated the Blood to cause the chaos and they needed to call in the Red Army when the Fox dies. You fell into their trap when you attacked the so-called Blood headquarters," I said.

"Why make another mistake?"

"CRML didn't get the documents when they killed Milos and Silvie. They have to attack in the next few days or you'll print the documents, right? So we're going to hit them first, mess up their command center, and give you the time you need to get the documents printed." There was a deep silence.

"Okay, let's go," said one, and the argument was over.

We pulled up across the street from the address that Igor had given me. I was planning to go up with them, but there was no elevator. With my leg, climbing stairs would only slow them. They piled out of the car and carried the guns into the building. I checked my watch. When they had been gone three minutes I went around to the trunk and got the shotgun. It was only a four-ten, but it would have to do. I'd seen the fire escape and knew they'd try to use it. It was better I stayed downstairs; maybe the idealists wouldn't have the heart to do what had to be done.

Eight minutes after they had entered the building the shooting started. It didn't sound like much— tiny firecrackers popping in the distance. Only a single passerby even looked up to see what was happening. He walked on. There was another response when I pulled out the shotgun and leaned against the car. I put the chock on full and lifted the gun to my shoulder. I wasn't looking forward to firing the damn thing, not with my broken ribs. My timing was good; two guys leaped out onto the fire escape. I planned to let them come down at least a flight so I could get a better shot. But they turned and fired into the room, so I opened up. The first grabbed the side of his head and screamed as if he had gotten a bee in his ear. My second shot splattered into the man's gun hand.

I put a couple of more shots into them before two more guys came out. They had some warning and came out shooting at me, but they only had pistols. All their shots went wild. For the first time on my mission I had range advantage. I used it. It was more pathetic than glorious, though. The bastards got caught in the crossfire between the dissidents and me. They couldn't even defend themselves.

I listened to the pellets make singing music as they ricocheted among the iron grates of the fire escape, singing a tinkling song of death. Three of the dissidents came running from the building. We bolted for the car and got out of there as quickly as we could. One of the dissidents in the back seat with me was shot up badly. He coughed up blood and before we had gone three blocks, he was still. We parked the car and split up, but I hobbled along with Andrej for a block while he told me what had happened.

As they entered the building they had knocked out the only guard and had taken his keys, but they never had to use them. CRML had been confident of their invulnerability. Someone had opened the door when Andrej knocked, even though they didn't know him. They pushed in the door and started shooting. It was the right place, all right. There was communications equipment everywhere, a rack of automatic weapons on one wall, and even some Blood literature and police uniforms. None of the CRML people made it to the rack. It was shotguns and surprise against pistols.

I was glad to hear all of this. There was, of course, a chance that Igor might sucker me, but I didn't figure that was the case because I thought I understood his motivation. They weren't likely to question him too closely when he told them I shot those CRML agents, not with his long, illustrious history at the KGB. But the chaos caused by a big shootout like this one would help him make sure his tracks were buried deeply. Igor was in Minsk, a few thousand miles away, when the second attack took place.

I said goodbye to Andrej and got a cab. I told him he had to leave Zagreb, that a couple of those guys on the fire escape were alive and could recognize him now. I had no idea whether this was true, but it would give him an excuse to make his exit. He had done his share. I had a feeling that despite our efforts a lot more people were going to die before those documents got published. Katrina was glad to see me, but she had a question.

"You did it anyway?" she asked.

"Yes, the CRML command post. It will buy time." She seemed subdued, not angry as I had expected her to be.

"We must talk," she said. I nodded. "Some more of our people have been killed. Two have disappeared, people who knew the details of our plans to publish the papers. The Belgrade courier will arrive tomorrow morning, but the woman who was to take the documents to Skopje and publish them has disappeared. I was going to tell you to go ahead and leave tomorrow. You're going to Dubrovnik?" I nodded. "I'll go with you. I have a friend there who has agreed to carry the papers to Skopje."

"Good," I said, watching her carefully. She seemed both upset and tired.

"I don't know how I can go on with this, Nick. People are dying all around me. I'm tired. Our position here in Zagreb has become worse. They say my father is failing and that I should return to Belgrade immediately."

"We'll take a drive down the coast," I said. "You need a chance to catch your breath. I can take the papers to Skopje."

"No, with everything falling apart, I want to make sure you take the film out of the country. My friend Janos will handle things." I didn't argue.

We went over a few details. I was glad to hear we would be leaving for Dubrovnik in the morning.

Suddenly we were interrupted by shouts and yells. We went to the outer room. A guy was kneeling in the middle of the room, blindfolded with his hands tied behind his back.

"We caught a spy, a traitor," said one of the gun-toting guards. Another put his shotgun to the man's head.

"Let's shoot the son-of-a-bitch," said another. By now a half-dozen people had gathered in the small room.

"How do you know he's a spy?" Katrina asked.

"Better take him into the other room," I said. We waited while he was hauled off.

"Jan, how do you know he's a spy?" Katrina asked.

"Well, at this point, he has confessed. The Blood paid him to spy on us."

"How did you catch him?" I asked.

"Well, first he told us how involved he was in Kosovo and then he lit up a cigarette."

"Lighting up a cigarette is hardly proof he's a spy," I said. Suddenly I found six pairs of eyes staring at me and a shotgun shifting in my direction. Katrina quickly stepped toward me.

"Everyone knows what Nick has done for us," she said. "He knows not to smoke, but he wasn't told why." She turned to me. "It's a little trick we have. The inner circle have agreed not to smoke. Every once in a while a guy like this turns up claiming to be an insider and the first thing he does is light up a cigarette."

"Let's shoot him," someone said about the spy. "He's not even a believer in the Blood."

"He's a goddam mercenary," said another dissident. "Let's put a bullet in his brain."

"That seems a little too hasty," I said.

"He will get us killed if we let him go," said Jan.

"You gain nothing by killing him," I said. "Why not trade him for some of your people?"

"What if they won't trade?" Jan said.

"Then we'll have to let him go," Katrina said.

"Well, it's settled." Nobody said anything, so I figured it was. She slipped her arm in mine.

"Let's go in the other room and talk," I said. Out of the corner of my eye I saw the dissidents push the spy toward the door.

"You know," she said, "just when I think you have no morality you speak up and help save that man's life."

"Yeah," I said, "that kind of relates to what I wanted to talk to you about." I paused a moment.

"Listen, Katrina. It's going to be win or lose in the next few days, but either way you'll be killed if you stay in Yugoslavia. It's not a rational thing, you understand. CRML *should* forget about you even if they lose and wait quietly to see if the chaos they wanted to produce artificially develops naturally. But they won't, and they'll kill you. CRML is so vicious that even some of the men who work with them, like the KGB, are uneasy. Come with me. Once we're finished in Dubrovnik I'll get you aboard an American submarine."

"Nick . . . my father. I have to go to Belgrade after I deliver the papers."

"Okay, Belgrade then. We can still pull you out. I'll come back for you myself, but you must be careful."

"Nick, I—"

"CRML is going to go insane when they see everything they worked toward all these years destroyed by you. You'll be safe in America. I promise you that." I was actually looking forward to her coming to the States. I think she sensed that.

She looked at me tenderly. "My father needs me; I must return to Belgrade. My country needs me. Let's not talk about different worlds anymore. It just makes me sad."

I looked at her but said nothing. She was right, of course. Tomorrow evening I would be in Dubrovnik, and the next night I would rendezvous with the U.S.S. *Stone Crab* fifty miles off the coast.

I led her to the bedroom and closed the door. The others had gone, but I wanted privacy. We undressed each other. Later we fell asleep in each other's arms. The dreams were vivid, brightly colored, and lasted a long time.

CHAPTER XXII

We were up early the next morning. Katrina made her usual phone calls. Even listening to only one end of the conversation, I could tell things were not going well. There had been more raids by the police against both the Blood and the dissidents. The newspapers said nothing about this, and the big local story was about the failure of a refrigeration unit in a Zagreb ice cream factory. I had a laugh when I saw that little item. The controlled press never ceases to amaze me. The entire rest of the front page was devoted to the Fox, and it was clear the population was being prepared for his imminent death. He had lapsed into a deep coma and his vital signs were failing.

Katrina's father had taken a severe turn for the worse. Her secret contact at the hospital, a nurse supervisor she had known many years, told her she should return to Belgrade immediately if she wanted to see her father before he died. Katrina was becoming increasingly frazzled. She paced the floor between calls and became a bundle of nerves. Meanwhile I studied the map and drank my Turkish coffee. I thought I'd figured out the best possible route to Dubrovnik, but Yugoslavia isn't the

U.S. and there weren't many routes to choose from. I had found a little-traveled turnoff that would get us across the mountains to the Dalmatian Coast. After that, there wasn't much I could do, since there was only one road along the coast. It ran right along the Adriatic Sea.

If anyone were to learn of our plans, it was this stretch of the trip that would be the most dangerous. There were almost no turnoffs or connecting routes, and the road was narrow so it would be easy to set up roadblocks. I had tried to impress upon Katrina exactly how vulnerable we would be if our friends from CRML and OZNA learned where we were going. But there were a lot of calls and many people involved, and although they used a code and played some tricky games with the telephone lines they were basically amateurs. I had little confidence our plans couldn't be discovered.

I checked Wilhelmina and put extra clips into my jacket pocket. I went down and checked the car, a boxy red Yugoslav-built Zastava 100. It was no Maserati, but it would have to do.

All morning our departure kept getting delayed by more phone calls and mysterious arrivals and departures. The Belgrade courier had reported that she was being followed and had to run for cover. No one knew if she was even close to Belgrade. Suddenly there were a lot of tearful goodbyes and hugs and I found myself walking arm in arm with Katrina down the stairs to the street. I looked at my watch; it was nearly ten o'clock.

"Nick, I'm sorry we're so late. There are so many loose ends still untied," she said as we drove off.

I assured her everything would be fine. We sat in

silence for a long time, then she said, "I don't know how much more of this I can take. Sometimes I think I am losing my mind. You're always so cool and organized, I don't know how you do it."

"Experience," I said. "I've been doing this for a while. You need to rest and get away from all this." I still wanted her to come to the States with me, but I didn't say that just then. She slipped over next to me and put her arm around me like a high school girl.

"We can stop at the Plitvice lakes for lunch," she said happily. "Have you seen them? It is the most beautiful place in the country."

I shook my head. I didn't care one way or another about the lakes, though stopping might help Katrina's mood. It sounded to me from the nurse's reports that her father had about had it, and we had a tough two days ahead of us.

We drove southwest toward the coast. The mountains grew higher, and large, thick forests replaced the farmland. The country grew more and more beautiful. But as beautiful as it was, the countryside didn't prepare me for the lakes. We parked the car and Katrina got out the lunch. Scenery aside, I was glad to stretch my legs, and with no breakfast I was nearly as hungry as I had been when we hadn't eaten in the mountains.

There are sixteen lakes, each spilling into the next lower lake by way of waterfalls and cascades. I had seen a lot of scenery up until now, but nothing quite like this. There were few people around except for several tourists and some fishermen. I waved to one old man and he showed me a string of trout and a half-toothed smile. I had already walked away, when he came up and gave me four

fish wrapped in white paper. I tried to politely refuse him, but it was no use, and he wouldn't take
any money either. He said he didn't fish that much
and just liked catching them.

The lakes were surrounded by the biggest trees
I'd seen in Yugoslavia; some must have been a
hundred and fifty feet tall. We ate our lunch and
drank our wine next to a small waterfall. Katrina
finally relaxed. I imagined this was what the real
Katrina was like, where she belonged. She looked
at me, and with a smile she said she was feeling
better and was ready to leave.

Instead of continuing on the main road, we
turned off to remote Lika Valley into the tiny village of Gospic, where Katrina tried to call the hospital to inquire about her father, but she got no
answer. I turned on the radio for the hourly bulletin on the Fox. There had been little change in his
condition.

We climbed up the steep, winding road from the
lush, fertile valley to the spine of the rugged Velebit
Mountains. As we neared Halan Pass, suddenly, as
if by magic, the forest ended and the barren, chalky
hillsides began. I pulled over. We could see miles
and miles of the Kvarner Gulf before us. The sea
was a bright, sharp blue sprinkled with olive-green
and cream-colored islands. I studied the winding
highway down the coast. Descending the chalky
mountainside was like entering another world as
we moved from primordial forest to the coast,
which reminded me of the south of France.

Soon we were on the famous but narrow highway running south. The mountains were now miles
behind us and the landscape rich and flat. We
stopped at Zandar, an ancient city. It had been

heavily damaged by German bombing during World War II, an all too common occurrence in Yugoslavia, but appeared well restored. I looked around a bit while Katrina made her calls. People were clustered around radios everywhere, in front of shop windows, cars, and when I went into a store to buy some wine there were a half-dozen people just standing around listening to the latest bulletin. For them, the rest of the world had stopped.

When I returned to the car I found there was no news. Katrina's friend didn't answer, and the Belgrade courier had still not shown up. The road south continued along the flat plane, but the landscape was dotted more and more by olive orchards and vineyards. Katrina sat in stony silence beside me, her cheerful mood from earlier a thing of the past.

As we approached Split I watched Katrina grow more and more miserable. I myself was feeling a little apprehensive and beginning to think about stepping aboard the U.S.S. *Stone Crab* without Katrina. I wanted her with me, not stretched out cold in some morgue full of holes.

When we reached the ancient Roman city of Split, we noticed that everything was draped in black. The Fox was dead. People were still clustered around radios but this time they looked gaunt and numb. Some were crying, but most just looked stunned. There was funeral music on all the stations. It would take them a while to adjust. The man who had led them right or wrong for forty years was no more. The Fox had gone to join all the other great leaders.

Katrina had me listen to the radio while she went

to call. She wanted to know if the Fox had made his promised announcement endorsing the dissidents. There was no mention of it, maybe because they were still playing music. But if it turned out he didn't endorse them, I wouldn't be surprised. I'd never believed he had any intention of doing it. That was just too much crow for the old Fox to eat.

Katrina came back to the car looking haggard. There was still no word about either her father or the Belgrade courier. The radio went into great medical detail about the history of the Fox's illness. Any normal man would have died six months earlier. Still watching little clusters of stunned people moving about like zombies, I pulled out of the city. I hadn't seen anything like it since the Kennedy assassination.

"I have always opposed the Fox," Katrina said, "but it will be strange without him. I hope we can have a country without a dictator and still not tear one another apart." I just nodded and kept my eyes on the narrow, twisting road. Frankly, bigshots come and go and unless they get you into a war and get a lot of people killed, the world goes on more or less the same as before.

It was beginning to cool. A few small clouds lay on the western horizon. We drove through an area of small fishing villages that had turned into resorts, called the Markarska Riviera. The beaches were small and scattered among piles of rock. Katrina insisted we stop so she could phone.

When we finally reached the port of Ploce, she made her call and stayed on the phone a long time. She came to the car absolutely stony. I figured she'd gotten the news, but I didn't ask.

Soon we were driving through a swampy area

and she said, "The courier has finally arrived in Belgrade. My father is dead. He died just two hours before the Fox. The nurse couldn't get away sooner without attracting attention." She stared into space. "I can't believe it, he is dead." Then she broke down sobbing and I looked for a place to park. I spotted a small, rocky turnoff a minute or two later and pulled over. I made her get out and walk a bit, even though she was making horrible, desperate sobs. We looked out over the Adriatic Sea, which looked beautiful. I said little, but I held her and let her crying run its course. When she was through, she turned resolutely and got back into the car. Again, I had to admire her strength.

We were making our way south when I began to get a funny feeling about the yellow car on our tail. Maybe it was the way it was driving, or the size of the passengers. I made a quick, last-minute turnoff to the town of Ston on one of the few side roads off the highway, and the Fiat whipped on past. Either I was wrong or he had lost us. I drove into town and parked at the square near the famous Church of Saint Michael and kept watch for the car. After fifteen minutes I drove back to the highway; we had no other choice. This was our only route.

I skidded out onto the highway and pulled up behind a big diesel truck. There was no sign of the yellow Fiat. Pretty soon, though, I began to get that funny feeling about the guy on our tail. This time it was a green Fiat, with three guys crammed into it. I pulled off the road at Treteno and circled around the small park. I ripped around the square, scattering tourists like a flock of pigeons and then hit the brake. When my fellow sightseers in the green Fiat pulled around the corner, I put a single slug into their right front tire. The Fiat twisted and slapped into the sides of two parked cars. I grunted with satisfaction and hopped back into the car.

"They are probably waiting for us down the road—more of them, that is," I said to Katrina, who had remained silent all this time.

"How could they find out so quickly?" she said.

I looked at her. "We may never find out," I said. "But what is certain is that they want us very badly, and right now."

I pulled back to the coast highway. I was glad Katrina was coming back to life.

"How well do you swim?" I asked.

"Not well enough to swim to Dubrovnik, if that's what you have in mind." It was still half an hour's drive to the famous walled city.

"I was thinking of Kolocep."

"The island is too far, Nick."

"We'll stick to the road then," I said.

I concentrated on the driving. We wound our way down the rocky coast. Most of the time we were high above water, between sixty and seventy feet. Suddenly I saw something.

"Look, a roadblock," she said. Damn! I knew the yellow Fiat hadn't just disappeared into thin air. There it was, blocking the road with a gray police car. Apparently CRML had connections with the local police, too.

They must have seen us coming because they began driving toward us. I pushed the pedal to the floor. The Zastava did all it could. We plowed through to the sound and smell of ripping metal. I knocked the yellow Fiat in wobbly circles toward the cliff, but it didn't go over. They turned the car around and came after us. I wove in and out of traffic, but they came up right behind us, taking even more risks than I did. The next thing I knew, the guy riding shotgun had opened up on us. I barely heard the sharp cracks of the pistol over the roaring engines. The back window shattered into thousands of pieces. Katrina ducked, then pulled her own gun. She twisted around as best she could and opened fire. I wondered if she was just aiming for the car. Then our front windshield splattered in front of me. I waited for a blind turn, pulled over to the left, and hit the brake. I spun the wheel hard when the Fiat, surprised by the move, pulled up next to us. Our right side cracked into their left hard. There was a terrific jolt, and we started spinning in circles. I fought for control. For a moment I didn't know whether it was them or us that was going over the edge, but then suddenly we slammed into the embankment. The car twisted so that it pointed in the direction from which we had come. The abrupt stop threw me hard against the wheel, but I turned in time to watch the yellow Fiat tip and slide gently over the edge.

Our Zastava was in bad shape, but when I turned the ignition it started right up and we drove the last sixteen miles to Dubrovnik rattling like a collection of tin cans headed for a recycling mill.

We ditched the car on the outskirts of town. Our suitcases had been shot full of holes, but we dragged what was left of them out of the trunk and tried to disappear into the throngs of tourists as quickly as we could. I noticed that Katrina was carrying the trout.

CHAPTER XXIII

Dubrovnik is actually two cities, an old city completely surrounded by massive stone walls and a newer, outer city that has grown up around it and is now filled with tourist hotels. Cars are allowed in the new city, but only a few delivery vehicles are driven within the walls of the old city, for the simple reason that the streets are too narrow except for the Placa—the main drag. Because of its spectacular location and because it is considered the best preserved medieval city in the world, Dubrovnik is one of Yugoslavia's main tourist attractions. During the spring and the summer, when its festival of plays, dance, and music is in full swing, Dubrovnik is thronged with thousands of tourists from dozens of countries. For this reason I had chosen Dubrovnik for my point of exit. There could be no better cover than the thousands of milling tourists.

We took a bus from the outskirts of the city, where we had dumped the car, to a park near the old city. We got out here to have a long talk. Katrina was very shaky and sad and finally after a long argument agreed to leave with me if her director friend Janos Nemcek agreed to deliver the papers to Skopje and organize their publications. She agreed to come for only a few weeks, "to rest," she said. She was worried she had become a kind of walking death warrant for anyone who helped her. Maybe it would be better, she agreed, to let others do the work for a while. And if she left for a while, CRML and OZNA would waste a great deal of time looking for her. This, too, would be good. She would come if Janos agreed to take the papers to Skopje. That was a big if, but I felt a rising excitement that she would stay alive instead of ending up a patriotic corpse.

We walked through the ancient gate of the old city and wandered the narrow cobblestone streets until we found the address where Katrina's friends were staying. They weren't there when we arrived, but we left our suitcases with a woman who said they would be back soon. Although we hadn't been there too long, I didn't like the looks of the place. There were too many doors and windows, and it was on the ground floor. Katrina grabbed the satchel with the documents and we headed off to the theater to meet with the director.

Dubrovnik is one of the most remarkable cities I have ever seen. I figured that once much of Europe looked the way it still did—narrow, twisting streets, stone buildings, plazas and fountains all surrounded by massive stone walls to keep out the many enemies. Dubrovnik was once a great city state like Athens. It had ruled a large section of the Dalmatian Coast and had a fleet of ships that plied the Adriatic. It also had a republican form of government when almost everyone else had forgotten what that was, and it had abolished slavery three-hundred years before the U.S. did. Then suddenly it became a backwater and lost its population. Because Dubrovnik was bypassed by the industrial revolution, it remained the way it was until the scholars and tourists rediscovered it.

They were rehearsing when we entered the hall. Katrina pointed out the director to me, and I grabbed a seat about two-thirds of the way back while Katrina went to talk to him. They were doing Shakespeare's *Coriolanus,* to my mind the best of the great bard's plays. It sounded strange in Serbo-Croatian.

After the director made some adjustments on stage, Katrina went up to greet him. He jumped off the stage and gave her a great hug and placed a generous kiss on her mouth. Something told me at one time they had been more than friends. After talking to him a couple of minutes, Katrina came back and plopped into the seat next to me.

"He'll be finished in a few minutes," she said.

"Great," I said.

She seemed happier than since she had heard the news about her father. I slid my feet over the seat in front of me and relaxed, listening closely to the bard's words. It wasn't too long before Katrina's director friend came down the aisle toward us. Katrina rose to meet him. They stood in the row in front of me deep in conversation.

"Oh, Nick, this is Janos Nemcek," she said.

I pulled myself to my feet and shook hands. He was a man of medium height with a broad, pleasant face and gray eyes. He looked neither intimidating nor authoritarian, but I had heard the way he ordered his actors around.

Katrina was telling him about the manuscript. He seemed uneasy, and I sensed he might refuse.

She was engrossed in her description of the documents when he interrupted her.

"Did they kill Ivo Mudrac?" he asked. "There is a rumor going around."

Katrina didn't hesitate or try to soften the news. "Yes, we think they murdered him."

"And they ran over your father? Katrina, if they killed Ivo Mudrac, a Lenin-Prize winner, they wouldn't hesitate to kill me, and I have a wife and two children now. I know what I told you over the phone, but I didn't fully realize the situation then."

"But Janos, you're from Skopje. You're the best person to organize publication there." She then told him the president of Skopje was one of the controlled ones.

"Katrina," he said, "I can give you names. . . I'll think it over, but I don't know."

I couldn't blame him. If he got involved in publishing this particular set of historical documents, survival over the next few months weren't too good.

"What about your father?" he asked.

"He died this afternoon a couple of hours before the Fox. I guess they are holding back the news in order not to interfere with the ceremonies they plan for the Fox."

"He was an incredible man, Katrina. I am very sorry. I don't think I am brave like your father . . . or you. I just want to direct my plays and live in peace. Let me think it over. I will tell you tomorrow night. We'll arrange to change a line in the play. If it's changed, I'll do it; if not, then I cannot. Do you know Coriolanus's speech where he says, 'Call me a traitor, thou injurious tribune! Within thine eyes sat twenty thousand deaths, In thy hands clutched as many millions, in thy lying tongue both numbers'?"

"Yes," I said. Katrina nodded.

"If the actor says 'ten thousand deaths' instead of 'twenty,' then I agree. But let's not meet again. I have a special place, however, where you can hide the documents. Come, I'll show you." We walked back stage.

"How many of these plays of ours could you direct if it hadn't been for people like Katrina's father?" I asked.

He frowned and bit his lip.

"That's not fair, Nick," Katrina said.

"No, he has a point. I'm thinking about that. Here, I'll show you," and he knelt down and pulled out a panel of wood from the wall.

"Here is where I keep my treasures, plays that will probably never be produced, by writers who will perhaps never be published." The cavity in the ancient brick wall was filled with ragged-edged manuscripts.

"We practice scenes from them sometimes," he said. "If I was in the West the big-money men would probably tell me they're not commercial. Maybe they are no good anyway, just junk, but I guess I'll never know."

Katrina said: "If we keep the Stalinists from handing us over to the Red Army, there'll be time for society to change, Janos."

"Katrina, I don't believe CRML can hand us over to the Russians. Yugoslavs would fight. We have all those weapons stored in the mountains, and the whole army is trained in guerrilla warfare. And don't mistakenly think the many nationalities want to return to murdering one another again, despite what the cynics say."

"You may be right," said Katrina, "but I prefer not to wait and see."

Nemcek carefully replaced the wood door. "Ah," he said. "Here, I have one for you," and he pried open another door. I looked in; it was empty. "I had a new one built," he said. "I have so many plays now, I need more room. But it's safe. No one knows about it so far but the carpenter and I. And the Fox had the carpenter's son shot, so . . ."

It looked okay to me, so I put in the briefcase and we said our goodbyes.

The timing that night would be tight. I had planned to go the play but we'd slip out early. The boat was scheduled to pick me up at ten o'clock. With the gates guarded we would have to go over the wall, which seemed easy enough—if they didn't see us going up. From the other side of the wall to the ocean was just a few feet.

After leaving the theater we went to the end of Stulina Street, where we would go over the wall. An old, beat-up tin can was stuck in a crack in the ancient wall. I pulled it out, and a scrap of paper slipped into my hand. It was from Rosa, my contact. In simple code it said, "All set," and gave me her hotel room number and telephone. She had been given the details of my present rendezvous once she had relayed my message to Hawk. I looked around carefully, trying to appear the good tourist. Everything looked fine. It was getting dark, and we had to race to one of the entrances to the wall and pay our fee quickly so we could get a look at the exit spot before the wall closed for the night.

We strolled along the top of the wall. It was a long way down, but that didn't bother me; with a rope it would be easy. We walked all the way around the wall studying the town carefully and then headed back to the apartment. When we were within a block of it a figure emerged from the shadows. I slipped my hand into my jacket.

"A friend," Katrina said. The tall, thin young man approached us nervously. I glanced around.

"Katrina," he said, "someone has been asking about you. One of my roommates was approached by someone he thinks works for OZNA. And there is a story going around that you are wanted for questioning in connection with the death of a member of the Blood during a street riot. The word is that if you turn yourself in and answer a few questions, everything will be okay."

"We can't go back to the apartment then?" she said.

"It may be watched," he said.

"What about our luggage?" Katrina asked.

"We'll smuggle it out piece by piece tomorrow. If there is something special you need . . . but I think this is what you want." He handed me the four trout wrapped in paper and gave a knowing grin. "Microfilm hidden in the fish, right?"

"Something like that," I said, taking the trout as carefully as if they were stuffed with diamonds. I smiled at Katrina.

"I guess we can get by," she said. "We'll let you know about the clothes."

Katrina had some other friends we could stay with—four women sharing an apartment. Unfortunately they already had three friends staying with them, which made the sleeping arrangements kind of public. There was room, though, to fry the delicate trout. We shared a bottle of Yugoslavian riesling and found places on the floor to sleep. It had been a long day, but tomorrow would be longer still.

I woke to the clatter of women—eight of them in a small, two-room apartment. It's lucky I'm fond of the female sex or I would have gone bananas before getting out of there. It was like being in a crowded, chaste whorehouse.

Katrina's tall, skinny friend arrived. He kept looking at the ladies while he whispered that the other house had been surrounded by police this morning. "They told everyone they were searching for drug smugglers. The whole town is full of police and OZNA," he told us. We saw him off and made ready to leave. In a hurried conference we agreed to disguise ourselves and separate, but we would keep in sight of each other the rest of the day. Katrina left for the theater. I waited ten minutes and then followed her.

It was a nice, clear morning, but the first thing I noticed was that the police were everywhere. I casually made my way to the theater.

It was locked when I arrived. Katrina was standing nervously in front of the door. I picked the lock, and we slipped back to the dressing rooms. Then I helped cut Katrina's long blond hair into a page boy and helped her dye it black. After I sprayed my fake mustache a distinguished-looking gray, Katrina and I gave it a conservative, Germanic-looking cut. I added ten years to my age with make-up and gave myself a small scar on the cheek and spent half an hour getting a nice, trimmed gray beard in place. I went to the theater shop and cut the heel of my right shoe at an angle just enough to create a slight, barely noticeable limp.

When I got back to the dressing room, Katrina

was putting the finishing touches on her make-up. She looked like a different woman, but still beautiful, though I felt bad about the long blond hair lying on the floor. I watched her wander around in her blouse and panties looking for the right dress. She found an old-maidish print dress. I put on a colorful tourist's outfit—a blue leisure suit with a bright yellow shirt and a phony gold chain around my neck.

We left the theater in our disguises and stopped to get something to eat at a local café. Even while I sat there I could feel the town fill with goons and police. When we finished breakfast we remained seated until I saw the tour groups beginning to make their rounds.

Then we got up, and watching each other closely so we didn't get our signals crossed, we joined separate groups about thirty feet apart. Once when the groups were close enough I heard Katrina getting her lecture in French. Mine was in German and Italian.

We toured the Rector's Palace, probably the most impressive building in the city. The rector was the man who ran the city on a rotating basis for only a month. He couldn't leave the palace while he served. Most of the lecture that accompanied our tour was long and erudite. I smiled bleakly at an old man and his wife who seemed almost as bored as I was. He nodded, and I started up a conversation with them. I noticed that Katrina was deep in conversation with a middle-aged man. From the Rector's Palace we went to the Dominican convent, Sponza Palace, and finally down the main street, the Placa, to the Franciscan convent.

Each of these places was filled with great art, but

the places between them were filled with OZNA and police. I must have walked past two hundred pairs of watchful eyes during the course of the morning.

In the chapel we caught up with Katrina's group. It was obvious to me that she was scared. The reason wasn't too hard to figure out—she had three goons following her. I hadn't expected anyone to spot her. One of the goons had sharp eyes, and it would be best to close them permanently.

As the place began to clear out of both groups, I caught her eye and gestured for her to take the side door to the restrooms. I said goodbye to the old couple and promised to meet them for lunch. Katrina slipped out the door. The goons hung around a minute, uncertain what to do, then followed her. I hung back in the shadows.

As soon as they had gone through the door, I ran over and opened it a crack. There was a long, wide hallway beyond, and the goons were standing around in front of the ladies' room talking quietly. A couple of little old ladies came out. When they reached the side door, I stepped back and pretended to look at the statue of a saint.

When I went back to the door I saw the goons moving for the ladies' room, pistols drawn. I leaped through the door like a leopard. Two of the goons had already entered the ladies' room. The backup saw me and at the last moment turned his pistol in my direction, but Hugo, biting deeply into his throat, cut short his intentions. In almost the same motion I pulled Wilhelmina.

Shots rang out, and I pushed through the ladies' room door expecting to find Katrina lying on the cold concrete. One of the goons was looking up and firing at a window high over the toilets. I stuck Hugo deep into his back and twisted. The second goon turned and started shooting, but in his excitement he plugged his friend, who was still in front of me. I shot him in the forehead.

I dragged all the bodies into a broom closet next to the ladies' room and covered them with old rags and newspapers. Then I raced back to the ladies' room and climbed out the way Katrina had obviously gone. I slipped my head and neck out of the window and pushed myself through. When I landed on my feet, Katrina was right in front of me.

"What happened to those men?" she asked.

"They've seen their last ladies' room. Let's get out of here."

"I hope there won't be any more of this," she said. "They tried to shoot me when I climbed through the window."

"Don't worry. We'll leave as peacefully tonight as tourists." But as we hurried through the streets we saw even more police than before.

CHAPTER XXIV

I went to a crowded café for lunch. Katrina sat by herself directly across from me a few tables away looking unhappy. I thought that she might be thinking about her father, but I really didn't know. I wasn't especially cheerful myself, but I had a practical reason. Ten goons were scattered around just this one café, and there must have been a dozen cafés in the area.

After lunch we resumed our sightseeing. All afternoon the walled city filled with more police and plainclothesmen. CRML must have been going all out to nail us even at the risk of tipping its hand. They were taking chances bringing in so many players who weren't in the know.

Everywhere I looked, there were the wrong kind of eyes, searching, but not finding. And I was standing right there, hiding in plain sight. If they dumped any more goons into the place they would end up blocking one another's view. Even the tourists had begun to notice. There were stories out about a drug-smuggling ring. People complained about being searched and questioned when they tried to come in or out of the walled part of the city. I noticed guys walking the walls with automatic rifles, and I heard no tourists had been allowed up on the walls since noon. Someone said it was because they were making repairs.

Late in the afternoon when Katrina's tour and my own drifted close together for a minute, I mouthed the word "theater" to her. I had had about as much of this as I could stand without taking a look around. I walked down to the end of Stulina Street to look over our exit once more. Dubrovnik has two gates; I strolled by them both. There were a dozen policemen at each, searching everyone coming and going. And goons of one type or another were hanging around. I wasn't in the city of Dubrovnik, I was in the prison of Dubrovnik. It wasn't going to be a departure tonight; it was going to be a breakout. The place was swarming with tourists, and I figured a lot of innocent people were going to get hurt.

I took a long, slow walk around Dubrovnik studying the streets and buildings more carefully than I had done before. When I had finished I looked around for a crowded bar, somewhere the goons might figure I was one of their own sneaking off to bend an elbow. I still had an hour and a half before theater time and I wasn't in the mood for dinner. I pushed my way up to the bar and ordered a vodka straight up.

While I was waiting for my drink to come, I took a look around. Goons everywhere. Three of them were standing with me at the bar, but between us was a tall blond woman. She gave me a big smile and started up a bit of conversation. I picked up on it—failure to do so might've aroused the goons' suspicions.

She wasn't beautiful, a little too finely chiseled in

the face, but she had quite a figure. Her tight black pants didn't leave much to the imagination. She leaned up against me invitingly. I could see this was going to get sticky. I don't think she saw the obstacles to our relationship that I saw. I looked at the clock; it was time to go to the play. The thugs at the bar gave me envious leers. I was a bit of a hero, I suppose, for picking up one of the beautiful foreign ladies. I told my lady friend that the goon next to me was a rich man looking to spend his money. She turned immediately to the goon on my right and started paying him special attention. He didn't mind. I quickly headed for the door. They never noticed.

The streets were still filled with police. I walked down the Placa and took a detour to look at the wall again but stayed far from where we planned to go over. I saw only a couple of men with automatic rifles. They must have figured the wall itself would be enough to stop anyone from escaping. Having seen something I liked for a change, I went to the theater.

The crowd was international—American, English, German, French, Eastern European, Asian, and OZNA. There were particularly a lot of the latter. If a room filled with goons didn't scare the director, I didn't know what would.

I didn't see Katrina when I looked over the crowd, but I saw Rosa. For a while we just stood a few feet apart, not saying anything. She was quite a handsome woman. We looked around the place together, following each other's eyes. I think we understood each other perfectly. She was carrying a large tennis-type bag with her. I figured she had brought along some heavy weaponry. The doors opened and I moved in to find my seat. I sat down a little uneasily. I was getting worried about Katrina. Then this strange, dark-haired woman came in and sat down in the seat in front of me. It took me a moment to realize it was Katrina. She gave no sign of recognition at all. That was the way I wanted it.

There were goons on either side of the stage and a pair at each exit. I searched the audience, trying to make my gaze casual. We had a lot of company, all the wrong kind. Finally the lights went down.

I sat back and forced myself to relax until the first act was over. When the end of the act finally came, Katrina and I joined the throng heading for the door. The half-moon-shaped lobby was packed with people. There were three pairs of doors, each packed with goons. I could imagine what the situation was like outside the doors. For the first time in days I was worried. I wasn't sure we were going to make it out of Dubrovnik alive. I looked at Rosa standing a few feet from me, her long black hair wrapped up around her head. Her role tonight would be a dangerous one. I didn't like it one bit.

I walked back in with the rest when the lights signaled us. I took a last look around the lobby. I knew during the next intermission things were going to be tight. I had been wondering about whether Katrina would be coming with me, but now I began to worry if I could even get her out of there alive.

This time I whispered a few details of our exit to Katrina. I walked down the carpeted aisle and took my seat. It wasn't too long into the second act, when I noticed somebody staring at me. The side of his head was patched up and I thought I knew his face from Zagreb. I looked at him out of the corner of my eye. He gestured to his buddy. I had definitely been spotted. He kept up the stare hoping I would bolt. I saw him carry the message to the rest of his pals but they did nothing. After a minute or two I leaned forward slightly and whispered. "Be ready," in Katrina's ear. Then I sat back and watched the play.

Somehow the line went by without my catching it until the end. I heard "in thy lying tongue both numbers." I had worked my way back, playing the half-heard line over in my mind. "In thy hands clutched as many millions." Then, "Within thine eyes sat ten thousand deaths. Call me a traitor, thou injurious tribune!" "Ten thousand!" I thought. She was coming with me. I noticed Katrina relax as if a weight had been removed. I waited for the curtain. When the lights went up they started to move toward me.

But the crowd was on its feet just as quickly and already milling toward the doors. I took Katrina's arm—no more discretion was needed. I caught Rosa's eye. She waited at the end of the aisle until we had passed and moved in behind us carrying her tennis bag. The goons didn't hurry. All doors had been alerted now, I figured. I could see the guy with the patched head point me out. They probably didn't see how we could get out, and I wasn't so sure how we would either.

I looked at the side exits as we moved through the crowd, but if I stepped out of one of those doors I also might step into a half-dozen guys with automatic rifles. I kept pushing for the lobby and whispered to Katrina that we were going to make our move. I looked back through the crowd.

Rosa's head was bobbing in and out of a sea of faces. I kept looking until I caught her eye; she blinked that the message had been received. I didn't have any detailed plans as we moved into the lobby, but I drew Wilhelmina and slid her into my jacket pocket. I'm tall, which is an advantage; I could see more of what was happening than most of the goons, not to mention the civilians.

Just before we entered the lobby a guard at the end of the aisle made a grab for me. I stuck him with Hugo, deeply, but missed the heart on the first stab. I twisted Hugo out and tried again. This time I was right on the mark. Katrina saw it happen out of the corner of her eye and made a slight wince, but she said nothing.

The lobby was packed, and the thugs were waiting for me. I saw them pushing through the crowd from three different directions. I had to think fast.

"So many, Nick," Katrina said quietly.

"Count your steps," I said. "Concentrate on your feet. It's an old trick." She smiled at me. "After we get out of the building, don't run in a straight line, and try to keep sideways to the shooters when you can." She looked doubtful.

"You'll be all right," I said. I just hoped she wouldn't be too nervous to aim straight.

They were getting close now. I studied the doors. There was no way through them without shooting. I didn't know how I could get a decent shot in the undulating crowd, and then it hit me. I remembered the little leap for the window I had made in the ladies' room that afternoon, and as soon as I remembered it, I acted. I leaped as high as I could, swung out Wilhelmina, and shot the two thugs standing in front of the right door. The recoil knocked me a bit off balance as I came down. Then I put a couple of slugs in the ceiling. The crowd panicked. I screamed "fire" several times as loud as I could and the crowd hit the doors like an avalanche. The goon behind me to the right opened up right into the crowd, the cowardly son-of-a-bitch. I jumped up, just to put a bullet down his gullet, but I couldn't get a clear shot.

The screaming, terrified crowd poured out of the doors and surged down the street. We tried to stay in their center. The street was filled with a line of police and OZNA shining spotlights on the crowd, but I don't think that made what was happening any clearer to them. It just frightened the crowd more.

We stayed with the center of the crowd for half a block. The police and OZNA scattered to side streets to get out of the way. We heard shots. Somebody had opened up on the crowd, seemingly at random. When I looked back, I saw both the crowd and the police line but couldn't tell who was shooting. In twenty feet we'd break free of the crowd and be visible. We sped up and emerged from the mass at a run—and shooting. Some policemen tried to block our way, but I put away the first one with a single shot in the gut. I clipped the second one on the side of the head as we ran by.

The police and OZNA opened fire. A lot of innocents started taking bullets. I caught another thug in the eye with a kiss from Wilhelmina; he seemed to be shooting blindly. He spun dead like a toy top. Another gunman dropped flat on the ground and opened up on us. I returned fire but couldn't get a clean hit. I fired and fired, but the guy was too damn lucky. I emptied Wilhelmina at him and still he was shooting back unscathed. Suddenly his body twitched three ways at once. Rosa had caught him with her Skorpion. I seized this opportunity to put a fresh clip into Wilhelmina.

A goon moved from behind a post and opened up at less than ten feet away from us. I pumped two slugs into him and watched him fall. The bullets kept coming quicker and quicker. I grabbed Katrina's hand and swung her forward. "Run!" I screamed. The bullets were splattering around us now, tinkling on the cobblestones like hard-iron rain.

In twenty yards we'd be around a corner. I turned and emptied Wilhelmina at our pursuers and saw a few more men hit the pavement. Then I saw Rosa running desperately about thirty yards behind us. I sprinted toward the protection of the corner and reloaded.

Katrina rounded the corner first. There were bullets everywhere, almost all of them headed in our direction. Just as I turned the corner I swung Wilhelmina around and put slugs in the direction of our closest pursuers. One guy doubled over and another grabbed his side. Then I passed around the corner out of sight.

Katrina was already halfway down the block. I twisted around to watch the action, but kept moving at a jog, waiting for Rosa. The rain of death was growing thicker. I heard two bursts from Rosa's Skorpion. She came around the corner in her black dress, her black hair flying, at a sprint. But she took the corner a little wide and was still a good target. She looked at me. I caught her eye just as a submachine gun opened up on her. She caught a full burst and was lifted right off the ground. Her arms flew out helplessly in different directions. When her body fell to the pavement, I knelt down next to her. She gave me a vague smile and with her last strength she tried to motion us on. She was trying to tell us to get out of there. Suddenly her body went limp. I stayed there one stunned second but Katrina's cry brought me into action.

There was nothing to do but run. Katrina had reached the end of the block, but in the confusion turned right instead of left. I cursed our luck. When I reached the cross street I saw her running frantically back toward me. Two guys with carbines had opened up at the end of the darkened street. A dozen of the thugs following us had already rounded the other corner. The two riflemen seemed the biggest threat, so I decided to take them out. It was long-distance shooting and it took five shots but I silenced them. It was time to run again.

I turned down the next short block and turned left once again. The wall! I pulled out the 9mm climbing rope I'd bought in Zagreb and tied it around my waist, unwound it, clipped on the hook, and swung it up over the wall. A gunner on top of the wall opened up on me. Katrina shot him. I pulled the rope taut when the hook had caught and said, "Climb!" to Katrina. "I'll hold them."

I went back to the end of the corner while Katrina started climbing. When I reached the corner I threw myself on my stomach. There were two dozen men running down the block toward me, some in uniform but most in plainclothes. Some had carbines, some pistols, some carried submachine guns. Only my arm and head angled around the corner. I waited until they got close and then opened up, hitting the first five guys in a row,

one after another, like shooting ducks in a shooting
gallery. Then I emptied the clip into the rest, slid in
a fresh one and kept firing. A lot of guys didn't
make it back to the other end of the block. They
fell one after the other. They tried to shoot back,
but I wasn't much of a target.

When Wilhelmina was empty and they had scattered, I turned and ran for the wall. Katrina was
almost up. I reloaded; I was almost out of ammunition. A bullet splattered near me. Another guy on
top of the wall was shooting at us. I picked him off
with two shots. Finally Katrina made it up and I
followed like a monkey. Our pursuers rounded the
corner and opened up on us just as I dropped behind the battlements.

"I didn't mean to shoot him," Katrina said. "It
was an accident." For a moment I didn't know
what she was talking about; then I remembered.
She had never killed before.

"It's all right," I said. "Remember, Katrina, it
was him or us."

I could see a couple of guys running our way
around the wall. I got up and looked seaward.
Below us was a red speedboat. I waved and someone waved back. I grabbed the rope and pulled it
up. The wall that was supposed to keep us in was
now an insurmountable barrier to our pursuers.
They pumped a lot of lead into that stone wall, but
all I did was walk over to the other side and let the
rope drop down. I helped Katrina over the side,
then turned and took care of one of the guys still
running around the top of the wall to get us. The
second guy, watching what happened to his buddy,
lost his nerve and ran for it.

I went over the wall feeling a tremendous surge

of relief as I swung down the stone face and hit the rocky base. The boat was just a few feet away and I climbed in to join Katrina in the back seat. "You'll like the U.S.A.," I said, reaching over to reassure her. Then I turned and looked up at the massive wall of Dubrovnik.

"Nick, I'm not going. I can't," she said.

I turned and looked at her. "Of course you can. You'll be killed if you stay."

"I can't go. This is my country. This is what my father fought for. I can't leave while everything is happening." I tapped the driver on the shoulder to signal him to take off.

"You have to go now," I said.

"I can't." She pulled out her pistol and pointed it at my gut. It didn't mean what it seemed. I knew she wouldn't shoot me. I looked at her long and hard. She was right; this was her country, her home. I knew I had to let her go. I leaned forward to the driver. "The quay," I said. "We have a passenger to let off, if we can do it safely."

"Yes, sir," he said. It must have sounded like suicide to him, but he didn't argue. I was back among pros.

For all the chaos in Dubrovnik, the quay was quiet. A few tourists strolled among the fishing craft and yachts.

"No more Western technicians in our country, Nick."

"I'll tell them," I said. "That's all I can do." I looked at her. "You won't change your mind?"

"You're very sweet, Nick, but I can't."

"Pull over," I told the driver.

"Anything I can do? Anything you need?" I asked. We pulled alongside the quay. No one paid us any attention. I held my hand up so she could use it to climb out of the boat. When she took it, I held her a minute. It took all my years of training to let her go. She climbed up.

"Oh, Nick," she said. "Here." She reached out and handed me twenty bucks Yugo.

"What's this?" I said.

"Buy yourself a caraboose steak in remembrance of me."

"I will," I said. I reached out my hand once more and she took it.

"Take care of yourself, Jesse James," she said, and then she turned and walked away.

"Let's get out of here," I said to the driver. "There's a patrol boat coming." I didn't have to say another word; he let it rip—full throttle. The patrol boat tried to intercept us as we left the bay, but we were too fast. We picked up another, faster one a few miles out to sea. I pulled the M-60 out from under the back seat and rigged it up and let them have a long burst out of range to let them know to keep their distance. Soon we were cruising in international waters.

An hour before sunrise we had reached the rendezvous point. I watched the U.S.S. *Stone Crab* surface. The crew came up on deck and saluted me. Then the captain came up to confirm his instructions. He saluted and addressed me as "sir." I was back in the U.S.A.

The next morning I took off from a NATO air base in Italy, flying my own Phantom. I pulled out east over the Adriatic and cruised along the Dalmatian Coast thinking of Katrina. The Adriatic looked bluer to me than ever. The day was cloudless. I wondered how it would all end. I

banked west and checked my watch. I had one re-
fueling stop. In a few hours I would be in Washington.

Again I thought about Katrina. It would be a
long time before I went back to Yugoslavia. Right
now I was doing Mach 2, high, very high over the
blue Mediterranean.

POSTSCRIPT

The documents incriminating the "controlled ones" and their CRML masters were never published, but they served their purpose. OZNA raided both the dissidents and the Blood and seized all copies of the documents. But instead of being CRML's great victory it was their undoing, because the contents of the Nazi documents leaked to the Fox's loyalists in OZNA. They seized control of the organization and confronted the controlled ones, who were arrested and forced to resign. The OZNA head threw a suicide party about which there were many sad obituaries in the papers. But the Fox's regime was not Stalin's, and within a few months the dissidents, Blood, and CRML were released from prison but kept under the watchful eye of a reformed OZNA.

Even dead, the Fox was the cleverest and toughest Yugoslav of all. He had turned the greatest threat to his regime into one of its greatest victories. His enemies had been set at one another's throats—Stalinists, dissidents, and fascists. When they had drawn each other out of hiding and had mauled each other badly enough, the Fox's boys moved in and picked up the pieces. For better or for worse, after his death the Fox's succession went exactly the way the Fox wanted it.

Katrina had been a brave and wily lady. She lasted almost six months, but then disappeared. I was sure she had gone into hiding. I could not believe that she was dead. I promised myself I would go back one day and find out. Besides, I owed her some money. I still haven't found a place that serves caraboose steaks.

Yours truly,

Nick Carter

FROM THE

NICK CARTER

KILLMASTER SERIES

☐ TEMPLE OF FEAR	80215-X	$1.75
☐ THE NICHOVEV PLOT	57435-1	$1.75
☐ TIME CLOCK OF DEATH	81025-X	$1.75
☐ UNDER THE WALL	84499-6	$1.75
☐ THE PEMEX CHART	65858-X	$1.95
☐ SIGN OF THE PRAYER SHAWL	76355-3	$1.75
☐ THUNDERSTRUCK IN SYRIA	80860-3	$1.95
☐ THE MAN WHO SOLD DEATH	51921-0	$1.75
☐ THE SUICIDE SEAT	79077-1	$2.25
☐ SAFARI OF SPIES	75330-2	$1.95
☐ TURKISH BLOODBATH	82726-8	$2.25
☐ WAR FROM THE CLOUDS	87192-5	$2.25
☐ THE JUDAS SPY	41295-5	$1.75

 ACE CHARTER BOOKS
P.O. Box 400, Kirkwood, N.Y. 13795   N-01

Please send me the titles checked above. I enclose _____.
Include 75¢ for postage and handling if one book is ordered; 50¢ per
book for two to five. If six or more are ordered, postage is free. Califor-
nia, Illinois, New York and Tennessee residents please add sales tax.

NAME_____

ADDRESS_____

CITY_____STATE_____ZIP_____

NICK CARTER